WHERE THE
IRISES
BLOOM

WILL LOWREY

Where the Irises Bloom

Editing by Lana Mowdy
Cover by Rebeca Covers
Formatting by The Book Khaleesi

ISBN 978-1-7329399-4-3 (paperback)

Published by Lomack Publishing

LOMACK
PUBLISHING

www.lomackpublishing.com

First Edition

TABLE OF CONTENTS

To the lost souls who wander among us
— on two legs and four.

"Though we travel the world over to find the beautiful, we must carry it with us, or we find it not."

Ralph Waldo Emerson

CHAPTER 1

FROM THEIR SANCTUARY in the shadows, the rats scratched feverishly at the rotted under-belly of the floor that rested precariously above the damp, musty crawlspace. Their long teeth chipped flakes of decaying plywood to the sod-den ground below. Hidden in the far corner of their dingy lair, Percy and Fern huddled to-gether in the blackness as long spiders and fat, round beetles scurried nearby.

Hours had passed since Mother left the dark confines of this wretched place in search of food. It was unlike her not to return before the moon rose to its peak. Percy nestled closer to Fern, his coarse, gritty fur bristling against hers in search of solace.

Across the crawlspace, the rats scraped in-dustriously at the subflooring, seeking entrance to the abandoned house above. The last vestiges of sunlight receded through the broken wooden door to the crawlspace, and the shadows stretched long and deep beneath the feeble house.

Percy pushed closer to Fern; she could sense the fear welling within him. His narrow ribs trembled against her side, and his soot-black fur rippled. Fern nuzzled her chin against the top of his head to comfort him. Despite being the same age as her brother, she had always been the brave one. When Mother left the crawlspace in search of food, she entrusted Percy's care to Fern in unspoken silence. For several long hours now, they had huddled side by side in this dark corner. The other creatures of this dank catacomb, seemingly unmoved by their plight, had largely left them to face their fears unmolested.

Each night since they had been here, Mother would leave the crawlspace in search of food, often returning with the tiny carcass of some mole or wren to share with them. But Fern knew that this time was different. In her heart, she could sense that, somewhere out there, Mother was in trouble. Never before had she failed to return before the blanket of darkness fully cloaked the sky and the crawlspace succumbed to the inky black of night. The prospect of spending the night alone in the crawlspace chilled Fern to her core.

WHERE THE IRISES BLOOM

In the looming shadows, she rose from the muck and grime. The faint light from the waxing moon reflected off her speckled, calico coat. Beside her, the dark weevils burrowed deeper into the muddy ground. Her nostrils twitched with the smell of rot and mildew.

She poked at Percy with her nose, rousing him to stand. On shaky feet, the small, black kitten stood, cloaked entirely in the shadows, a specter in the darkened corner except for his green-yellow eyes that now looked upon the world in terror. Fern knew they must look for Mother. She locked eyes with Percy, her words unspoken yet clear, and then stepped lightly toward the broken door of the crawlspace as he followed close behind her.

Just then, the air beyond the broken door cracked with a sharp popping sound that pierced deep into Fern's tall, broad ears. She winced, and her body tensed. The walls of the crawlspace seemed to tremble for a moment, and then all went still, the sharp sound receding to a vacuum of cold silence. Fern stood motionless in the darkness. Beside her, Percy wobbled on shaky legs as if he might fall. She regained herself and perked her ears — listening, stretching her keen senses beyond the threshold of the broken door.

In the far distance, the night sky carried the faintest sounds of human voices, shouting and laughing. It sounded like men gathered near the park. Fern lifted her front paw gingerly and stepped into the soft dirt, each pace careful and methodical. As she walked cautiously, she listened, waiting for the next sharp pop. After several steps, she turned and looked back at Percy. In the blackness, his light eyes shone from the depths of the crawlspace; his face was etched in an unmistakable expression of fear. Fern offered a hollow, reassuring look and beckoned him to follow. Cautiously, he began to step across the muddy crawlspace, his paws pressing deeply into the soft ground.

She poked her head through the broken door, her fur brushing against the jagged wooden splinters. Then she sat for a moment at the threshold and let her eyes settle on the falling night. Ahead, the backyard of the abandoned home stretched a short distance to a tottering, chain-link fence. The yard was littered with trash and debris — broken liquor bottles, faded fast food wrappers, scraps of rusted metal, syringes, and all sorts of other debris. In the far corner, a rusted children's swingset lay toppled on its side, the stanchion rusted and buckled beneath its weight.

From the houses on either side of the yard, Fern could hear muffled voices carrying on the night sky. To the left, the sounds of a television blared through a torn screen window, only vaguely masking the clanking of dishes and pots. The sweet smells of meat being cooked on the stove wafted across the yard and filled her nostrils. Fern rested on her haunches and inhaled, her hungry mind filled with visions of feasting on scraps of the unseen meal just beyond the window. To the right, she could hear shouts and angry voices — a man and woman arguing loudly in an upstairs apartment. All around the block, she heard car doors slamming, the crackling of radios, mingled voices in conversation, and the noise of a rusted bicycle. The city was alive.

Fern looked once more into the yard, scanning for raccoons or other creatures who might be lying in wait. Her sharp eyes cut through the night, searching through the bushes and behind the garbage strewn about the yard. After a moment, she stepped cautiously forward, her slight silhouette hunkered low across the open ground. Percy followed her without prodding this time, and the two young cats darted quickly to the chain-link fence, their narrow forms unseen in the blackness.

She paused at the fence, stretching her hearing above the usual din of the city for any threats or alarms. Hearing none, she turned toward the fence and took one long step through the narrow opening, pressing her body between the jagged hole and the bramble roots that grew through the diamond-shaped openings. When she had passed through, she stepped forward and perked her ears once more, scanning constantly for any unusual sounds — or for Mother. Percy slipped through behind her with ease, his bony frame barely brushing against the wire.

Ahead, the silhouette of the abandoned paper mill loomed like a dead monolith in the black night. As far as Fern could see, the dark shape of the blocky factory stared across the urban wasteland through its dead, broken-window eyes. She crouched low and angled towards the edge of the mill where the shadows were darkest.

Halfway to the building, she froze in her tracks, and Percy stumbled to an abrupt stop, bumping into her. From ahead near the old loading docks, her ears caught the whispering of human voices carrying on the cool breeze. Her wide eyes narrowed to slits and focused into the darkness. Just ahead, she could faintly make out two figures in the blackness. Her ears registered a woman's voice speaking softly then the rustle of coarse fabric and the jingling of metal coins. She watched the man's hand thrust in his pocket, digging deep along the leg of his pants. Then he reached out and handed the woman two pieces of thin paper that she placed in her dark leather purse. Looking quickly around the empty lot, she adjusted her top and disappeared around the corner toward the neighborhood as the man straddled a rickety bicycle and rattled away into the night.

Fern and Percy sat motionless in the shadows for a long moment, watching the humans leave. Mother had warned them that the old paper mill was treacherous. In their short lives, they had dealt with no shortage of human threats at this place, and Fern knew to be wary around these parts. As the clanking of the bicycle receded into the distance, she continued forward, sinking into the cover of blackness near the edges of the building.

Above, the dull gray sky had melded to dusty

black. The half-moon crested overhead, keeping solemn vigil over the dreary city for yet another night. From the east, a brisk autumn wind rustled the dried leaves on the scattered trees and rippled the fur of Fern's short coat. The cool breeze was tolerable now, but she knew that soon, fall would give way to winter and the bitter cold would arrive — unforgiving. Mother had warned of the coming winter, and thoughts of the approaching cold were never far from Fern's mind.

Beneath the faint stars, the two cats edged around the old paper mill, occasionally stopping in the blackness to listen and watch. High above, beyond the broken windows, they could hear nocturnal creatures stirring in the building — industrious raccoons who had found their way inside, persistent rats who seemed to be everywhere, and thousands of unseen bugs who scurried and burrowed in the floor and walls of the old, dilapidated building.

Fern and Percy had been inside the old paper mill just once. Early on, they had followed Mother one day up the wide loading dock. They sat and watched as her sleek, gray-black frame crouched and leapt to the ledge of one of the lower windows, walking nimbly on the thin, rusted metal window frame. Mother looked downward at the two, beckoning them to join her. Percy jumped first, scratching at the bricks with his claws as he missed the ledge and slid back down to the loading bay. Fern waited patiently while her brother tried once more, bending his tiny black legs and jumping straight up into the air. This time he missed, never even touching the ledge. In frustration, he gave way to Fern and stepped aside for his sister to try.

Fern had always been bigger and stronger than her brother. Percy was unquestionably the runt — small and wiry, his ribs always showing through the spiky tousled hair of his jet-black coat. His eyes were a sickly pale green-yellow and seemed to sag on his face as if he bore a perpetual look of consternation. Despite his physical shortcomings, Percy tried mightily at everything he did, and Fern admired him for it.

That day on the loading dock, it was her turn, though. She stepped to the same spot where Mother had made her jump — she always watched Mother, observing and learning. Bending her legs in a deep crouch, she sprung forward at an angle, landing softly on the windowsill next to Mother, tucking her legs to make herself smaller as she landed. Mother was proud of her. She tilted her head and nuzzled the side of her face into Fern's cheek, the deep thrumming within her throat not going unnoticed on the ledge that day.

From above, Mother looked down at Percy, standing on the loading dock peering up at his little family. With her eyes, she told him that they would be back. Then, she dipped her head and angled her body through a crack in the window, moving slowly to avoid scraping herself on the jagged glass. Watching her as always, Fern followed and they found themselves high on a concrete ledge above the dusty factory floor that sprawled out endlessly below.

Fern had never seen an indoor space so large. As far as her eyes could see, rusted iron machines dotted the concrete floor, covered in a thick layer of dirt and old cobwebs that fluttered in the stagnant air. Countless metal parts littered the ground, strewn among shattered bottles and soggy cardboard boxes. The sun filtered through a hundred panes of crusted, broken glass, lighting the warehouse in shades of pale white and shadowy gray.

Suddenly, Mother's ears perked. Far across the warehouse, a human figure shambled into the open light. As he stepped from the shadows, his deep, dark skin looked dusty and dry, as if he had crawled from the very dirt itself. His hair was matted and twisted, and a wiry beard sprouted haphazardly from his chin. The man staggered toward the factory floor, muttering sounds to himself, and then leaned against the concrete, sliding hard down the wall until he was resting on the floor. In silence, Mother and Fern watched him from their perch as he rolled up his sleeve, exposing a spider web of thick veins. From his pocket, he retrieved a syringe and held it up in the light. The shafts of morning sun beamed through the plastic tube, highlighting the amber liquid within. They watched as the man muttered, his words spilling meaningless into the void of the warehouse, and then plunged the needle deep in his arm.

His chest sagged, and his eyes rolled in his head. Just briefly, he smiled, his lips parting beneath the coarse beard, the gray-toothed grin visible from across the warehouse. After a moment, his lips closed and his head slumped back hard against the concrete, eyes open, and lolled for a moment, and then slumped sideways, carrying the weight of his body to the dusty floor.

They watched for a minute longer, and then

Mother turned and slowly angled back out of the window onto the ledge. She said nothing, but Fern sensed that she felt no dignity in watching a man die. As Fern always did, she angled out the window and followed Mother to the ledge. Below, Percy mewed anxiously, longing to join them. In answer, Mother dropped softly from the ledge, first lowering her front legs and then pushing gently off the ledge to land next to Percy. Fern followed, and in silence, the three left the mill and the dead man behind.

Fern had never been back to the mill since that day. Two days after she watched the man slump lifelessly to the warehouse floor, she saw red and blue lights flashing around the mill, their sirens quiet — a corpse bears no urgency. She had walked to the edge of the chain-link fence and stared across as the lights cast strangely-colored shadows around the giant warehouse. Emotionless, the men in dark uniforms entered the mill and returned, rolling the man's body in a sleek, black bag into the flashing machine. After that day, Mother vowed never to enter the mill again.

On this night, Fern pushed the thoughts from her head and circled around the mill, sticking to the comfort of the shadows. On the far corner of the massive warehouse, she stopped and waited with Percy once again pausing behind her. Without looking around the corner, she tilted her head and listened into the night.

In the cool evening air, the leaves rustled and crackled in the trees. Far beyond the sounds of the trees, the faint sound of vehicles resonated beyond the chain-link fence. She perked her ears once more and listened closer, and her heart sank. Just below the voices of men talking loudly ahead, she could hear her — Mother. Barely audible, her faint, troubled mewing carried across the distance to Fern's ears. She was injured and crying out for help.

Fern poked her head around the corner, scanning quickly for threats. Before her, the city park sprawled into the darkness, a tiny sea of cracked blacktops and haggard trees, dotted with the rusted toys of a children's playground and the bare iron of worn basketball rims. Sitting perched atop a picnic table, she could see a group of young men and could hear them talking loudly in harsh, profane words — laughing and yelling at each other in jest.

Fern reached out in the darkness for the sounds of Mother. The silhouette of the swingset loomed from the cracked pavement like some unwelcoming gateway. The scant leaves on the distant trees twisted and turned in the crisp, cold breeze. Fern listened again and could hear her, far across the playground toward the woods. She could sense Percy's fear behind her, but there was no time to waste. Swiftly, she darted across the asphalt, heading straight to the tree line. Behind her, Percy followed closely, his tiny legs pumping as fast as they could carry him.

"What was that?" she heard one of the men say far to her left as she zipped past in the blackness.

"All these fucking stray cats out here, man," said another loudly, then the sharp sound of metal sliding on metal.

"Get that one, too, bro," cajoled a third voice.

"I ain't shooting out here again tonight. Screw them cats," said the voice.

Fern raced to the sound of Mother, her ears tuned to her quiet mewing in the blackness. At the edge of the wood line, she found her, lying on her side in the tall grass. Her sides rose and fell in ragged breaths. Fern stood above her, and

WHERE THE IRISES BLOOM

Mother's eyes looked up at her in distress. Her mouth was wide open, and her rough, pink tongue dangled sideways over her teeth as she wheezed soft puffs of air. Fern pressed her nose into Mother's snout, letting her know she was there. Mother's eyes rolled sideways, connecting with Fern's. Then she looked beyond Fern and spotted Percy, and Fern could feel an almost imperceptible sense of relief fill her soul, as if grateful the two were together. Fern stepped through the tall grass toward Mother's tail. She could smell the bitter, rich scent of blood in the air. There, just above Mother's haunches, a dark, crimson stain marred her gray-brown coat, wide and sickly under the silver moonlight. Fern's heart sank. She turned and walked back to Mother's face and rested on the ground beside her, pressing against her as if the warmth of her body might heal the grievous wound. Percy circled from the other side and stood over Mother, his limp eyes dire and full of sadness.

Mother looked at Fern and blinked twice, then her eyes grew heavy. She seemed at peace now with her children beside her, and the jagged breath became faint but steady. Fern pressed her head into Mother's chest, attempting to stir her to life, but it did no good. Mother closed her eyes and breathed deeply. Her chest rose and then went flat, never to rise again. In the dim glow of the pale moon, Fern and Percy lay there in the tall grass, huddled against the warm body of their mother.

CHAPTER 2

THE LIVELY CHIRPING of morning birds rose from the barren branches of the red oaks scattered about the playground. At the edge of Fern's world, the first faint rays of sun crested on the horizon above the dark silhouettes of the shabby row houses. She and Percy lay there, pressed against Mother, her body long cold and stiff.

In the distance, the sound of a truck engine carried across the dawn sky, its thrumming motor drawing closer. Fern lifted her head from Mother's blood-matted fur and watched as a faded, white pickup truck, with chipped blue and yellow lines down the sides pulled on to the blacktop some distance away. As the truck rolled to a stop and the door opened, she watched an old, gray-haired man with dark withered skin in a dull blue uniform step from the truck and slam the door. With a wobbly, bow-legged gait, he walked to a nearby trashcan, lifted the heavy lid, and dropped it to the asphalt with a loud metallic clank. Percy's head jolted up from Mother at the sound, and he sat upright, his pale eyes nervous and wide.

The old man muttered to himself as he worked, noisily bunching the edges of the plastic bag and hoisting it over his shoulder then tossing it in the bed of the old truck. As the bag landed with a thump, he stopped and looked across the pavement, his eyes falling on the cats. From the distance, Fern could see the pink of his mouth as he stared agape, discerning the scene across the playground. His brow furrowed, and his eyes squinted as he looked toward them.

"What in the….?" he muttered and started toward the cats, hobbling along on his old legs.

Fern hunkered low, pressing herself against Mother's body. From the corner of her eye, she could see Percy instinctively starting to move toward the grove of red oaks but then stopping, as if unwilling to abandon Mother. The two cats crouched motionless, hoping the man would turn back toward the truck.

But, he did not. Circling around the pickup truck, he approached them slowly, slouching his shoulders as if trying to make himself less threatening. His eyes squinted tighter as he drew closer, his buckskin boots treading carefully on the asphalt.

With each step, the old man moved closer and closer. Fern did the only thing she knew. Stretching her mouth, she bared her sharp, white teeth and released a long hiss. Behind her, Percy shuddered and took two backward steps toward the trees. Fern hunkered low, her fur bristled, and her tail rose until it stood vertically. She stared at the man and hissed again. *Back away. Leave us alone.*

The man ignored her threats and pressed forward calmly. "Your momma hurt?" he said, studying the scene before him.

Fern hissed again, mustering her courage and stretching her mouth as wide as she could to bare her fangs. The old man took two more steps forward. Percy glanced at Fern nervously, beckoning her with his eyes to run, and then he darted toward the woods, his furry black shape bounding hastily across the pavement.

The man's eyes lifted as he watched Percy run. Fern stepped forward toward the man, her body crouched low, and once more she hissed at him. He looked down at her, seemingly unphased by her display of aggression, and continued his slow approach. And then he stopped just a few feet away. His squinting eyes relaxed and then drooped into an expression of anguish as he looked down upon Mother's lifeless form.

"She gone," he said somberly, looking dolefully at Fern, her teeth still bared at him. "Your momma gone, little one," he said with a kind sadness. Then he dipped his chin and shook his head slowly from side to side.

Fern knew not what the man said, but the kindness in his tone was unmistakable. Instinctively, she drew her mouth closed and crouched before him, staring ahead at his boots.

"Them damn hoodlums," he said scornfully. His eyes were glazed with anger. "Look what they done," he said, staring down at Mother's body. Then, he stood upright and looked around the park for a moment. Through the branches of the red oaks, the morning sun rose in the sky, the soft rays lighting the wrinkles around his kind eyes. "Damn shame."

Fern studied the man. Her pale, yellow eyes stared upward, and her neck crooned back to look at his face as he stood before her. As she studied his expression, she could sense the grief within him — genuine and pure.

He glanced back down at her and then squatted, lowering himself to meet her where she lay. Then slowly, he reached out his hand toward her. Fern backed away, shuffling backward and tucking herself into the wedge between Mother's tail and back. She twitched her nose and inhaled his scent — the mixture of rotten garbage, salty sweat, and the aroma of cheap deodorant.

"I ain't gonna leave your momma here, kid," he said to her, his hand still outstretched. "But you should go…before they get you, too." Then he rose to his feet and hobbled back to his truck, pulling a long plastic bag from the bed. Walking back to where Mother lay, he turned sideways and shook the bag open. Fern startled at the sound and moved toward the tree line. The old man moved close to Mother and hunkered down again, opening the plastic bag beside her. Fern hissed at him. Once more, he reached his arm out toward her, but this time, he gently swept at her, shooing her away.

"I don't want you to watch this, kid," he said, taking a quick step toward her. Fern stood and darted a few steps toward the trees. "Go on," he said, sternly. She could hear the insincerity in his tone. "Get out of here," he said, his voice rising.

He stepped again toward Fern to scare her away. "Go!" he bellowed at her, his voice breaking. The sadness in his voice belied his stern tone. Fern ran for the woods, tucking herself into the sparse thicket near Percy. From the trees, she watched him slide Mother's body into the plastic bag and carry her to the back of his truck. Then he climbed into the cab, looked toward the woods shaking his head, and drove away.

Hiding at the edge of the woods, knowing that Mother was gone, the world seemed suddenly larger and more frightening to Fern. The red oaks above seemed to loom endlessly into the pewter morning sky. Before her, the playground seemed to stretch as far as her eyes could see. The chain-link fence leading to the paper mill was nothing but a distant blur of crisscrossing wires. She crouched low and scanned the world around her, her eyes absorbing the newness of her reality. Mother was gone now, and they were alone.

Near her, Percy stirred in the thicket, uncertain

and afraid. He took two short steps to Fern and pressed his side into her. She could feel the trembling through his patchy, black fur and knew they couldn't stay here. Searching the playground for threats, her eyes fell on a solitary goldfinch perched atop the jungle gym. His gold breast stood boldly among the drab asphalt and the rusted metal equipment, and his tiny head tilted sharply, listening for the sounds of kindred among the trees. Fern closed her eyes and listened to see if she too could hear what he heard. Beneath the growing din of the morning city, she could hear the noises of other birds, nestled somewhere unseen among the trees, calling and talking to one another in their secret, magical tones. While the humans slept, the city was alive —and she and Percy were alive too, and they must stay that way — for Mother.

She rose from her crouch and scanned the distance once more. Seeing nothing of alarm, she stepped softly from the thicket onto the sparse grass edging the playground. Behind her, Percy paused and then followed. Cautiously, the two cats crept across the playground, slipped through the chain-link fence, and pressed their bodies tight against the sides of the paper mill, making their way back to the abandoned house. As the sun rose higher on the horizon, the sounds of life began to buzz around them — the rattling of an old muffler as some unseen human puttered around delivering newspapers, the sounds of car doors closing as the faceless people headed to work, the soft din of the highway far in the distance that carried far on the quiet air, and the sounds of small dogs yipping by back doors to be let back into their homes.

Cautiously, Fern and Percy circled the paper mill, finding themselves once again at the gap in the chain-link leading to the backyard of the abandoned house. They stopped, and Fern turned and looked behind them, wondering what horrors lie within the mill today. After a moment, she slipped through the chain-link and slinked to the crack in the broken door, stepping inside to the solace of the damp, musky blackness of the crawlspace.

They slinked to the familiar black corner where Mother had hidden them for so long. Around them, they could hear the rats scurrying, pushing their fat bodies through cracks in the foundation to escape. Positioning herself against the cool cinderblock, Fern felt the soft wisps of cobweb wrap around her face and shook her head to loosen it. In the short time they had been gone, a spider had claimed their corner. *Mother may be gone, but we are still here.*

For two days, Fern and Percy stayed in the dark corner, huddled together. They dozed occasionally, but mostly they sat there, wide-eyed and afraid, wondering what the world held for them and unsure of what to do. She was hungry, but she could feel that Percy was starving. The sharp edges of his ribs poked through his fur and dug into her sides as the crouched side by side in the blackness. Mother would not be back, and she knew they desperately needed food.

On the morning of the third day, Fern stood and stretched her legs. Percy looked at her, worried. In the darkness, his sagging eyes looked sad and desperate, like his spirit was lost. *I'm going to find food*, she told him with her eyes. Percy simply stared at her, hungry.

She walked across the crawlspace and headed for the broken door, following the shafts of light that bathed the dark mud just beyond the entrance. Stepping into the light, her fur looked drab and dusty. The rusty orange of her calico coat was dull and brown, and the white was a drab, faded gray. She poked her head through the doorway and searched the yard for threats. The morning was cool and brisk, and the sun shone down through leafless trees, painting the backyard in a palette of shadows.

Fern stepped from the crawlspace into the open and looked around. She knew there was no food in the paper mill. Mother usually went to the park at the end of the day, searching around the dumpster and picnic areas for scraps of food left by the gathering humans. But today was not a day the humans gathered and ate. Today was a day they got in their cars or on their bicycles and left the neighborhood, only to return as the sun fell.

She looked to her left. A short distance across the grass, the houses rose in bunches, grouped close together. The abandoned house sat separate from the others on a sea of dead, dry grass, like some leper cast from the lot. Fern looked into the backyards of the nearby houses — the metal laundry poles stood cold and rigid against the morning sky. She could see trash cans pressed against the sides of the homes, some brimming with colorful plastic bags that looked out of place against the otherwise decrepit landscape. Behind the houses, a long, thin stretch of trees separated them from the bleakness of the old paper mill.

Fern started across the yard, heading for the nearest house and its disheveled collection of garbage cans. She could smell the rot coming from them — the pungent scent of rotten meat scraps permeated the yard and filled her tiny nostrils. She was hungry but wasn't sure from the smell that what lay before her in the cans was even edible. As she approached the rear of the house, she heard the noises of people talking loudly inside. Hunkering near the edge of the house, she crept toward the trashcans. Just above her, she could see the ledge of a window, and with a swift crouch, she leapt silently on her young, strong legs and landed on the ledge just above the trashcans.

Just as she did, the trashcan below her erupted with commotion, rattling and shaking violently. From the shadowy depths of the can, a fat, gray-black raccoon scrambled up the side in a desperate, blind dash to escape. Like a rocket, he shot upward, a furry blur rising from the depths of the garbage and landing on the edge of the can. He paused for a moment and stared at her. Fern's eyes fell on his long, gray fingers, sharp with thick black claws. She tottered on the ledge of the window in fright as the raccoon gawked at her, opening its mouth wide to reveal a sharp row of teeth. Then, it scrambled hastily across the edges of the other trashcans and disappeared around the edge of the house.

Fern sat there frozen in terror, unable to move as the trashcans rattled to a rest below her. Then, she heard the metal side door fly open, banging hard against the side of the house.

"Get out of here!" yelled a man's harsh, gravelly voice at her as he poked his head around the door, inspecting the trash cans. At the shouts, Fern regained her wits and jumped from the window ledge, clearing the trashcans and sprinting across the yard blindly into the grove of trees. She darted through the undergrowth and slammed headlong into the chain-link fence, bouncing backward.

"You better stay out of my trash, or you're going to regret it!" shouted the harsh voice from the open door. She could feel his anger permeating across the yard, yet she only sat there in a stupor, unsure of where to go. She hunkered low in the thicket and shivered. The cold wind rustled the dried leaves and ran straight through her short fur.

WHERE THE IRISES BLOOM

The metal door slammed closed, and after a moment, the yard fell silent again. For a long while, Fern tucked herself low in the thin patch of woods and hid, wishing she could escape the world around her. As the sun crept higher in the sky and the faintest rays of warmth spread stingily across her dirty calico coat, she finally moved, inching her way back toward the crawlspace.

From the thicket, she looked upon the house. The flaking, green-gray boards seemed to wilt, slouching dejectedly toward the ground. The old house looked tired and heavy, as if it remained a part of this world only begrudgingly. The sharp edges of broken window panes glittered in the morning sun, and the shingles wore a drab, faded gray-white, their natural hue drained years ago from the persistent sun. Fern looked toward the broken door and strained her eyes to see into the blackness. She could see nothing. Her mind wandered to Percy, cowering cold and hungry in the dark corner. For a moment, she sought to return to the shelter of the abandoned house and comfort him, but there was no food there. They needed to eat desperately, and he was counting on her.

Her eyes scanned the yard again, and seeing

nothing, she darted toward the edge of the abandoned house. Once, many moons ago, Mother showed them a store down the block where the scents of food were strong. She would go there and search the dumpsters for something to eat. Pausing for a moment by the abandoned house, she listened for any signs of distress in the crawlspace. She could just faintly smell Percy, and she inhaled his fear and hunger. Then she dashed beside the house toward the front yard and across the narrow, quiet street and into another yard with a small, faded blue house, pressing herself against the cinderblock foundation.

In the distance, she could see the shape of the store. The squatty, red brick building with its black shingled roof stood in the middle of a small, asphalt parking lot. Beyond the large windows that flashed with neon signs and tattered advertising posters, she could see racks and racks of snacks and candies standing rigidly in the sterile glow of the long halogen lights. Cars came and went from the store, their tires stopping abruptly against concrete pylons, doors slamming, and loud music blaring from their bellies. Near the back corner of the store stood a large, blue metal dumpster. Mother had taken them here before to find food, and she knew this place well.

She watched for a moment as the cars stopped and the people entered through the double doors. Near the front of the store, two men stood with their backs turned to her in an animated conversation. After watching patiently for several long minutes, she darted from the edge of the house, down the sidewalk, and across the parking lot, her small, powerful legs propelling her forward as fast as they could go. She didn't even look toward the men, only focusing on the blue metal dumpster. And then she reached it, hunkering her body low to slither into the shadows beneath. Behind her, she could hear the men talking loudly, and occasionally, the doors to the store would open, and the sounds of music and laughter would push their way boisterously into the cold world beyond.

Fern stopped and sniffed around her, inhaling the smell of the food above her in the dumpster — a mixture of old donuts, rotten fruit, and half-eaten convenience store meals. Crawling to the rear of the metal container, she emerged safely in the narrow space where the dumpster met the short brick wall. She leapt on a metal lip of the dumpster and then again, reaching the top gracefully. Below her, piles and piles of white plastic bags, slick with grease and strewn with litter, were sprawled unceremoniously. She dipped her front paws over the edge and then dropped, landing softly on a bag, her paws poking small holes in the plastic. There was food here and lots of it.

Fern's nose instantly was drawn to the sweet aroma of fresh cheese, and she crawled across the top of the bags to a small cardboard pizza box, lying open like a mouth agape. Greasy chunks of hardened mozzarella lined the creases, and she began to lick at the oil, savoring the rich taste. Then she started to gnaw at the stale cheese, holding the cardboard down with her paws while she pulled with her teeth, savoring small chunks that peeled from the cardboard. Below her, she could smell morsels of greasy chicken. Following her nose, she tore open a thin plastic bag with her paw and dug side to side with her nose until she found her prize. She stuffed her nose into the bag and pushed straight down, grasping the edges of a napkin bundled with half-eaten chicken wings, and pulled them through the small hole in the plastic. Spreading them out before her with her paws, she nibbled hungrily at the wilted, grayish meat. Then she chewed at the wings, tearing chunks of dried chicken from the brittle bone. After a moment, she paused, looking up from the edge of the dumpster toward the faint blue sky. She needed to bring Percy here so he might eat.

Crouching, she jumped to the edge of the dumpster and stood there, staring out into the parking lot. They saw her before she saw them.

"There's that cat!" shouted one of the teenagers, his voice loud and brusque against the cool morning sky. Before she could react, a beer can hurtled through the air and smashed against the side of the dumpster, spraying cold liquid all around her. Fern leapt wildly into the unknown, landing hard on the asphalt.

"You gonna end up just like your momma!" yelled another teenager, and they all laughed at her. She darted across the parking lot blindly, and the tires of a car squealed and ground into the pavement, just missing her as she scrambled away from the store.

Behind her, she could hear the teenagers laughing and the sounds of the driver cursing at her. The world was angry. And so she dipped her head low and ran, sprinting straight down the sidewalk for all the world to see, bounding across the yard and pressing herself hard against the side of the abandoned house until she reached the broken door, gasping.

She twisted her body through the crack and slipped inside. The dank blackness was comforting. As she stood there in the musky crawlspace panting, her mind raced and spun, the hectic scene playing through her thoughts. Beyond the broken crawlspace door, the whole world seemed one great threat.

From the far corner of the darkness, she heard a soft meow. Percy's wistful eyes greeted her from the blackness —scared, cold, and hungry.

CHAPTER 3

FERN KNEW THEY couldn't stay in this neighborhood any longer. The world outside their meager crawlspace sanctuary was far too dangerous. Between the scavenging raccoons, the foreboding paper mill, and the angry young men, they wouldn't last long.

As dusk fell over the city, the two young cats crept to the edge of the crawlspace, and Fern poked her head outside, surveying the yard. All down the block, amber lights lit the windows of the houses as families gathered inside, huddled away from the looming winter. The wind whistled cold and crisp across the yard, pressing into the gap in the crawlspace door. Fern squinted against the bitter gale. She could feel the harsh weather coming, but they had to move.

Quickly, she darted across the yard for the chain-link fence, Percy following close behind her. They reached the thicket and cowered for a moment, listening to the sounds of the city. Down the block, a car engine raced, and tires squealed against the pavement. Two sharp cracks rang out — gunshots. The cats cringed at the sound, and Fern's mind wandered to Mother lying gravely wounded in the grass around the playground. In the distance, harsh shouts rose from near the convenience store. The neighborhood was tense.

Fern's only plan was to leave this forsaken place. She glanced at Percy, reassuring with her eyes, and beckoned him to follow. Then she dashed down the fence, away from the paper mill, bounding over thorns and small bushes and hurrying unseen through backyards. They ran for six blocks until the yards faded into a cracked mosaic of broken pavement that chafed their tender paws. Ahead, Fern could see the cars whizzing down a main road. Blurs of shiny metal and red and white lights raced in both directions, the muted sounds of music pulsing through the windows. To the right, she could hear the sounds of the highway. Cars moved swiftly, rushing north and south in an endless, unabated stream. The raucous sounds of the lively world frightened her.

They crept onward to the edge of the dark

parking lot, their bodies pressed against a concrete embankment. Suddenly, Fern heard the blaring sounds of a radio to her left and the squeaking of bicycle tires. She stepped backward, hiding in the shadows with Percy pressed against her. Just ahead, a rattling bicycle rolled by, and the static-filled sounds of harsh music crackled from a speaker strapped to the handlebars. The dark silhouette of a man sang as he pedaled, the off-key notes fading away in the night as he passed.

Fern poked her head around the corner. The road stretched straight into the dark city further than her eyes could see. Just ahead, she could make out the pale concrete of a bridge. As three men approached on foot, talking loudly and laughing, Fern and Percy cowered in the shadows beside the embankment. She poked her head around the corner and focused down the bridge. On the other side, she could see thick foliage jutting from the far end of the concrete. Beyond that, she saw a smattering of parking lots, businesses, and office buildings whose tall glass windows cast the lights of the city back at her like a mirror. It wasn't perfect, but it looked far safer than the neighborhood, and she decided they would go there. But first, they had to cross the bridge. As the men approached, they ducked back around the corner, unseen. For a long moment, they waited and then crept around the corner.

Slowly, Fern started down the bridge with Percy following close behind her. They had just crept a short distance when the sound of a person approaching filled Fern's ears as he turned the corner and headed in their direction, swaggering and muttering beneath a pair of headphones. Fern pushed back around the corner, and they hid once more in the shadows. She would need to find another way.

Beside her, Percy looked frightened. In the dim glow of the street lights, his black fur was matted and dirty, and his pale, green-yellow eyes looked lost and scared. Fern brushed her head under his chin to comfort him and rubbed her body sidelong against his, conjuring her last remnants of bravery.

Slowly, she slinked back down the concrete embankment the way they came and followed until it met a chain-link fence. Perhaps there was another way across the bridge. Percy trailed close behind her, the two sniffing at the fence for any scents and searching for an entrance.

WHERE THE IRISES BLOOM

Eventually, Fern found a small gap, pressed down on the wire with her paw and stood there, gauging the opening. They could fit. She stood waiting for Percy, who cautiously approached, and then she wriggled her way through the fence. Percy ducked his head and, with some effort, pushed through as well.

They found themselves standing in a thicket of weeds and bramble bushes. Fern moved ahead through the bushes and then planted her feet suddenly and stopped, tottering at the edge of a tall, concrete wall. Percy stopped abruptly behind her, brushing into her backside. The two cats teetered precariously in the darkness, staring wide-eyed across a great fissure. Some thirty feet across was another concrete wall and in between was a deep chasm filled with gravel and two long metal tracks that ran as far as their eyes could see. Some manmade contraption no doubt. *Why would the humans put up such a barrier?*

Fern realized that the concrete bridge they had just left spanned this great divide. She wondered whether perhaps there was another way across as she looked over the chasm — it was much too far to jump. Even Mother couldn't come close to clearing that distance, much less two tiny cats.

Percy stirred behind her, frightened. She turned and nuzzled him again. Despite the barrier that stood before them, she could sense a certain safety about this place. No humans would come through that fence, and any walking below in the chasm could never reach them perched so high. But the dilemma persisted — *how to cross to the other side?*

Fern looked in both directions. To her left, the concrete wall ran parallel to the strange metal tracks as far as the eye could see. To the right, the wall ran to the backside of the concrete bridge and then continued beneath. She thought that perhaps they could crawl across the backside of the bridge and reach the other side with the businesses, and offices, and the dense foliage.

She started down the wall towards the bridge, walking carefully atop the clean cinderblocks that seemed untouched by man. Her nose smelled only the scents of other creatures, and this place felt like a hidden sanctuary, as if no man dared tread here.

As they walked along the narrow wall, the

moon crested in the sky, casting a silvery glow across the strange landscape. Fern studied the backside of the bridge as they approached, seeking any sort of foothold that might lead them across.

And then suddenly, the whole world started to shudder. The walls trembled, and the chasm below filled with the squealing of metal grinding on the tracks and the rushing of an on-coming machine. Fern hunkered low, bracing herself against the vibrations, seeking a foothold on the quaking cinderblocks to leap to safety in the thicket. The whole wall seemed as if it might fall over into the chasm, and her mind filled with frightening thoughts. She crouched as the machine came ripping through the dark tunnel beneath the bridge, and at the last moment, she pushed off with her back feet, launching herself headlong into the bramble. As she landed, she turned and looked for Percy.

Her heart sank.

The little black cat hunkered low on the wall, frozen in fear. He stood on wobbly legs and took one step, looking toward Fern, and then raised his leg to jump just as the machine came hurtling through the tunnel. The whole world rumbled terribly. Percy's pale eyes grew wide and desperate as his tiny leg slipped over the wall and he slid into the chasm, his screams consumed by the roaring machine. His tiny silhouette vanished before her as if he had been consumed whole by the night.

Fern's eyes drew open in horror. The great machine whistled past, and after a moment, the bushes settled around her as the rumbling subsided. She rushed from the thicket to the edge of the wall and peered over, straining her eyes to see into the darkness below.

The moonlight cast a somber pall over the crevice, illuminating the lines of the metal tracks set against the pale, gray gravel. Fern searched with her eyes into the abyss, looking for any sign of her brother, but she saw nothing.

He was gone, carried away by the great machine.

She sat there on the edge of the wall, and her whole world seemed to crumble around her. First, Mother, now Percy. She had failed to protect him, and now she was completely alone.

All but invisible to the cruel world, Fern perched on the edge of the concrete wall and let out a mournful whine. Her heart was heavy, and her cries welled with anger at the bleakness around her. The tunnel echoed with the sounds of her sorrow, and the world seemed to go silent except for the mourning cat perched high on the concrete wall. When her body grew exhausted from crying, she stepped slowly from the wall and pressed herself deep into the thicket and curled into a ball, wishing that the night would take her too.

The next morning, the sun rose slowly, draped in the begrudging clouds that hung stubbornly in the sky. The cold winds whistled over the thicket, rattling the sparse, brittle leaves and rustling the world around her. She opened her eyes and woke to face the city — cold and hungry. Her body ached, and she longed just to sit there, consumed by the brambles, but she forced herself to her stand. Hesitantly, she crawled to the edge of the wall and scanned the chasm for any signs of Percy. Looking down the tracks as far as she could, she saw nothing.

For much of the morning, she walked beside the stone wall, looking down into the depths for signs of her brother. As the sun peaked in the sky, her heart sank once more, and she turned back toward the bridge, forcing herself to press onward.

She slipped back through the gap in the chain-link and moved down the concrete embankment, less cautious now, with little care if anyone saw her. Her meaning for existence had drained from her soul on the playground and now on the metal tracks. At the edge of the embankment, she turned and looked down the bridge. In the distance, the foliage bent and bristled at the cool wind, as if beckoning her across. Placing one paw in front of the other, she walked quickly across the bridge, her mottled calico coat plainly visible against the pale concrete. Beside her, cars whizzed past in the road, splashing muddy puddles into the air, and a wet mist coated her thin fur.

Fern stared straight down the bridge, focusing on the branches that jutted out from beyond the concrete. Ahead, she could see the road continue past the stoic red brick storefronts with their worn and tattered signs. Finally, she reached the end and turned to her left, ducking quickly into the bushes that poked through the chain-fence. In the safety of the branches, she stood there, taking in the scene.

Across a vast parking lot, a new office building rose, looking clean and neat against the otherwise drab city behind it. The sun glimmered off of its glass windows and reflected the pavement below. To her left, the parking lot continued on further than she could see, row after row of faded white lines painted onto the dull black pavement. To her right, the main road crossed the bridge.

In silence, she stood in the bushes and stared across the road. An old, abandoned tavern rose unceremoniously from a lot of weeds and dead shrubs, a relic from historic Colonial times. The windows were shuttered with green boards, and the old brick was weathered, worn by hundreds of years of northern weather. Generations ago, the old tavern would have been a welcoming sight, probably a lonely building in a small northern outpost. Over the years, the blight had swallowed the history, and weeds and weather engulfed the past, leaving only a dilapidated husk in its wake.

Fern studied the odd building. Her eyes fell to the old, wooden deck that lined the front, facing the road. Flakes of white paint peeled from the rails. As she looked closer, she saw the shape of a man sitting there, pressed against the wall, his dark skin barely visible beneath a thick, winter cap. His olive green coat melded into the dull brick of the wall as if he too had been consumed by the drudgery of the place. Motionless, he sat behind the railing, a large backpack propped beside him. From the distance, Fern couldn't tell if he was sleeping or even alive.

To her left, she heard a car approaching, and she turned toward the chain-link, searching for a gap in the fence, to move further from the road. To her relief, the fence opened several inches at the edge of the bridge, and she slipped through and ducked into the bushes. Straight ahead, she noticed a gap in the bridge —a narrow opening that seemed to lead to the innards of the structure. Liquor bottles, plastic snack bags, and all manner of debris were strewn about the opening. Curious, she dipped her head and poked her nose into the darkness, sniffing for any signs of humans or animals.

As she poked her head in, her eyes adjusted to the darkness, and she could see into the opening that stretched for several feet into the depths of the bridge. She could smell mildew and mold but sensed no trace of man or other creatures. Then she paused for a moment. Ever so slightly, she could feel a hint of warmth coming from the opening, pulsing from thick metal pipes that ran through the bridge. With one cautious step and then another, she stepped into the darkness, her feet crunching on pieces of rotted wood and candy wrappers, blown into the gap by the frigid wind.

Bravely, she pressed onward, deeper into the narrow opening. The walls were close on either side, just enough room for her narrow frame to pass. As she slowly walked deeper into the darkness, a soft, gentle warmth enveloped her, the metal pipes pressing out a faint, radiant heat that warmed the strange chamber. Finally, Fern reached the end of the opening as her nose brushed against a thick, metal barrier that blocked her path. She stood there in the warm blackness, some twenty feet deep in the bowels of the bridge.

All around her was darkness. The metal pipe hummed, and the heat felt comforting as it soaked into her coat. Outside, she could hear the muffled sounds of cars rushing by. Yet, here in the bridge, she felt protected. No man could fit through the gap, and she could smell no other animals except for the lingering scents of ever-present rats. She wasn't worried about them, though. She had spent her youngest days in the company of rats beneath the crawlspace, and now she worried only about dogs and raccoons.

She sat back on her haunches and rested, finally and unexpectedly feeling safe in the bowels of the bridge. Her mind wandered to Percy, and she winced as she thought of his last moments, carried away on the great, metal machine, his eyes wide with terror. She wondered too about Mother and thought of her lying there, suffering in the darkness. Her mind recounted Mother's expression when she and Percy had arrived and how it had comforted her for them to be there. Fern was glad they had found her in her final moments. Then she thought about the man who took Mother away in the morning with his plastic bag. Her mind was still puzzled by this strange mixture of kindness and insincere shouts.

For a long while, she sat there in the darkness, and the brief memories of her short existence raced through her young mind. She was alone in the world of man, at the mercy of his whims, buildings, and strange, frightening machines. It all seemed cruel and cold as she sat there in the blackness and reflected on the meaning of it all. Yet, through the trials and turmoil, she had survived. She had crossed the bridge on her own and had found this dark sanctuary of sorts. Tomorrow, she would set out for food. She vowed to Mother that she would not fail again.

CHAPTER 4

FERN CRAWLED TO the gap at the end of the bridge and poked her nose out into the world beyond. Small flakes of white snow drifted down slowly from the skies, coating the ground in a thin, dusty powder. In the depths of the bridge, she had slept comfortably, awakened only occasionally when the great machine barreled down the tracks below. Each time she woke to the sounds, she couldn't help but think of Percy. Somehow, it seemed deeply unfair that the frail, little cat was gone, vanished from this world by something so completely foreign to his senses.

In the parking lot beyond the edge of the bridge, a cascade of cars entered from the far street. The sounds of engines stopping and doors slamming filled the morning sky, replacing the quiet solace of early winter. All manner of people in their coats and ties stepped from their vehicles and fanned their large, colorful umbrellas as shields against the powdery snow. Sheltered from the world around them, they hustled through the parking lot and down the concrete bridge to vanish in anonymity into the tall buildings in the center of the city.

In the shadows of the bridge, none of them noticed Fern as she stood and watched them as her soft nose sniffed the freshly fallen snow, searching for scents of food. Her belly was hungry, and she longed for crusted cheese from greasy pizza boxes and the dry meat of half-chewed chicken wings. She was sure the food in the dumpster was long gone now, and even if it wasn't, she would not dare go back to that place. The young men, with their loud words and harsh tones, frightened her. They had taken Mother, and she knew to stay away.

She peered out from the bridge and looked across the street to the tavern. Her eyes fell once more on the shape of the man, his back pressed firmly against the wall. She could see him now in the morning light. His eyes were open and seemed to be watching the world pass him by, absorbing the morning people hurrying to work with an unblinking and dispassionate gaze. He looked the same as he did the night before, except now Fern noticed a drab, gray blanket wrapped around him. His black winter cap was pulled low, buried beneath a hood that shrouded his dark, weathered face. Curled wisps of a silver-gray beard covered his angular chin.

For a long time that morning, she watched him silently. He sat there motionless, as if only a spectator to the world. The working people passing paid him no notice as they shuffled by. Most did not realize he was even there. As far as they were concerned, he was a part of the decaying old tavern — no different than the weathered bricks or the paint-chipped shutters.

Fern stepped her two front paws out from the gap in the bridge and stretched, her body drawing a long line parallel to the ground. The pipes of the bridge provided a scant but welcome source of warmth, but the concrete beyond was hard and unforgiving, and her bones and joints ached from the long night's slumber. Above her, soft wisps of winter snow danced from the sky and fell on the crest of her head and melted on the bridge of her nose.

She had felt snow once before, just briefly. Shortly after Mother had given birth in the dark recesses of the crawlspace, she stood at the broken doorway, looking back at her kittens and meowed, summoning them. Fern and Percy waddled across the muddy soil, their coats damp and dirty, and drew near to Mother at the edge of the crawlspace. They gazed at the world outside and all around, small flakes of white powder fell from the sky, clinging to the wilted tops of the dying blades of grass. Fern stepped gingerly from the house into the yard and stared upward in wonderment. A blanket of powder fell slowly from the thick clouds. She felt the flakes land in her open mouth; the cool sensation of snow melting on her tongue made her body tingle. The snow was brief that day, and by the time the sun rose behind the soggy gray clouds, the hints of white powder had melted, leaving only the damp, dead grass behind.

Today, Fern knew the snow would not recede. She stared at the fat, dark clouds that consumed the drab city. They seemed to be overflowing as if the tufts of dark, gray cotton were bulging forth and expanding across the morning sky. She knew the snow would fall for most of the day ahead.

She turned and looked to her left, gazing down the long chain-link fence that stretched down a thin strip of grass edging the parking lot and followed the line of metal tracks in the chasm where Percy had been lost. Then she crept quietly from her lair and followed the thin row of small trees and shrubs that separated the chain-link from the chasm. Once more, she was hungry.

Following her nose, she hunkered low on the ground, stopping to sniff at the pieces of trash that littered the path. Ahead, her nose signaled a fresh salty smell, and she followed the line several paces away until she found a crumpled, brittle plastic bag of potato chips, exposing its guts to the world. She dug her nose in the bag, savoring the salty smell, and licked with her rough tongue at the corner; small flakes of chips and crumbs flicked into her mouth. The taste of the salt was sudden and startling. She sat up, licking her lips, her eyes twisting to discern whether she liked the taste or not. Hungry, she dipped her head back into the bag and licked the corner until she tasted no more. Then she stood there, staring down at the empty bag as if somehow her eyes might conjure more.

As she stood there, the plastic bag caught on a crisp breeze and tumbled empty across the asphalt. She turned and continued down the row of trees as a few more cars entered the parking lot and stopped, their engines running for several long moments before they ceased. The car doors opened then slammed shut again as they dispersed their human contents. The people paid her no mind. In fact, hidden behind a small berm of grass, she was quite sure that few even saw her.

She stopped along the way at every bit of trash. The smell of old liquor crinkled her nose in disgust as she sniffed at the broken bottles. Bits of paper napkins and plastic sandwich wrappers fluttered in the cold wind, devoid of any sustenance. The parking lot was vast, stretching the length of a whole city block. Standing atop the small berm of dead grass, she looked across the lot and could see another street to her right and, just across that, a giant brick building or theater of some sort. The building looked cold and formal, and she sensed no food there, so she continued down toward the far end of the parking lot where the chain-link fence bent to the right and ran the length of another road.

Above her, the snow began to fall heavier now, thick flakes landing on her coat and soaking into her fur. Occasionally, she shook herself, and moisture flickered all about in tiny droplets.

She paused for a moment under the gray skies and sniffed again. The scent of fresh tuna filled her nose, and she stood upright, focusing all her attention on the rich smell.

After a moment, she located the source and began to trot at an angle from the fence, into the parking lot. She stopped by the parked vehicles and hunkered low against their tires, listening and waiting to ensure she was not seen. The pungent hint of nearby food pushed her onward.

There, across the parking lot, she saw it. A clear plastic wrapper fluttered in the breeze, pinned against the concrete pylon of a street light. Fern looked left and then right and darted to the wrapper. Pressed against the corner of the open wrapper rested a small chunk of tuna fish and some remnants of bread from a discarded sandwich. She squatted and ate hungrily, chewing full-mouthed on the bits of bread and savoring the tuna as it melted on her tongue. But before she knew it, the morsel was gone, and she sat there once more licking at the empty plastic wrapper.

Her belly still ached with hunger, yet there was no more food here. Lowering her head, she sat there pathetically by the empty wrapper in the middle of the parking lot, hidden only on one side by the concrete pylon of the street light. The snow was thick and wet now, and it sank into her coat and chilled the tender skin beneath.

From behind, she heard the wheels of a car approaching, the slick black tires flicking a trail of moisture from the blacktop. The noise startled her and she ran, bolting across the lot to the chain-link fence where she cowered behind the small berm watching. After a moment, the car parked, and a woman emerged in a dark suit-coat and skirt. She popped a black umbrella and hurried off across the parking lot toward one of the big buildings of the city.

Fern waited until she was gone and then slinked down the chain-link fence back to the gap in the bridge. She would wait inside and warm herself by the metal pipe until the snow had subsided, and then she would resume her desperate quest for food.

As the low, brittle branches of the trees that shaded the entrance to her sanctuary brushed against her fur, she stopped and looked across the road at the old tavern. There he sat, motion-less, propped against the wall in his gray blanket. She stared at him from across the road, somehow drawn by his presence.

Fern knew he didn't have food. He didn't appear much better off than she was, but there was something that called her to him. She saw his eyes move, the bright whites set against his dark skin shifting to watch her. He looked at her, and their eyes connected, two homeless souls left to their lot on the streets of this forsaken city.

Without a thought, Fern stepped forward onto the sidewalk that ran the length of the concrete bridge. She looked left and then right and darted across the street toward the tavern. He watched her coming with emotionless eyes, like some sentinel only observing without feeling. She stood there for a moment in the dead grass at the corner of the porch, some twenty feet from the man. Through the rotted wooden railing, she could see his form there on the porch but could no longer see his eyes. From the distance, his pungent odor filled her tiny nostrils.

Sensing a bush to her left, she moved into it, shielding herself from the traffic on the road and from the man on the porch. She could not tell if he was watching her. From her vantage point, she saw his old, buckskin boots, their soles worn thin and gravel pellets lodged within the cracks. Beneath the old, gray blanket, she could see the edges of his thick, heavy pants and his olive green coat.

Fern watched for a long time, waiting for the man to move or threaten her like the others did. He never did. He only sat there quietly. The occasional noises of his breath pushing across the grass on the late fall wind were the only sounds in her ears.

After some time, she crept to the edge of the porch and looked up. She could no longer see him, hidden somewhere above the porch, but she listened closely and knew that he was still sitting there. Something drew her to him. Perhaps a longing for companionship, perhaps the hope that he would have food for her, perhaps his unthreatening nature, or perhaps the fact that here they both sat, alone and homeless.

Then, she tucked her legs and leapt on the edge of the railing, slipping through to stand just ten feet from the man. He did not move at her approach. His eyes only shifted to look at her, and she studied his face. His skin was rich and dark like cocoa, weathered from the toll of untold seasons. The white-gray stubble around his chin reminded her of the wisps of powdery snow fallen on the gray pavement. The drab gray blanket was pulled up to his chest, nestled tightly against his winter coat. On his head was a thick winter cap pulled tight against his skull, and by his side, the remnants of his world were stuffed into a tall backpack.

He watched her standing there, the whites of his eyes streaked with red and a tint of yellow. They studied her, and while she couldn't tell what he was thinking, he showed no fear and exuded no threat.

For a long moment, the two sat there on the porch of the old tavern with a blanket of snow falling around them, set in some uneasy truce. Fern rested on her haunches, signaling to the man that she would stay for a moment.

They gazed in each other's eyes for several long minutes, and then the man's left hand moved slowly from beneath the blanket. Fern startled at the movement and stood upright, edging toward the railing. The hand stopped for a moment and then continued, moving slowly and methodically, cloaked in a black, cotton glove. He reached for a zipper on the backpack and slowly pulled the metal buckle. The crease on the pouch opened, and he raised his hand slowly and patiently, reaching into the bag.

Fern watched as he pulled a long piece of colorful red and yellow plastic from the pouch. Her nose perked as she could smell the spiced meat that lay within. The man pulled the package to him and raised his other hand to his mouth, biting on to the fingers of the glove then pulling his hand loose to reveal his bare skin, weathered and rough. He reached up and fumbled with the wrapper, struggling to grip the small edges of plastic with his rugged hand. Finally, he grasped the crease and pulled the plastic open. The rich scents of the meat filled the porch and rushed into Fern's nostrils.

Fern's nose quivered excitedly, anxious for food. He looked at her twitching, and she thought his eyes softened and begrudging creases formed around his mouth as if he wanted to smile but had forgotten how. She looked into his eyes to study his intent. Sensing no threats or fears from the man, she sat there patiently. In her mind, she knew that Mother would tell her to run, to flee the porch and stay away from these people. It was people who had shot Mother and thrown beer cans and cursed at her. Deep inside, her instincts longed to run, but as she sat there in the presence of the man, cold and hungry, she felt a strange sense of peace

The man twisted the rich meat with his hand and broke off a large chunk, shifting it to his other hand. He held out the meat in his cal-loused palm toward Fern, still several feet away. She leaned forward, her nose taking great whiffs of the air. She could almost taste the meat through the winter sky, but she still dared not approach.

The man bobbed his hand up and down several times as if gesturing that he would throw the meat. Fern sat back on her haunches, waiting, and on the third try, he gently swept his hand upward, and the meat floated in the air, landing just before her with a thud on the wooden porch. She took her eyes off the man for a moment and looked down at the meat —a long, dry chunk of beef, the shape of a cylinder. Without so much as sniffing, she dipped her head and took the meat in her mouth and began to chew with her small, sharp teeth, breaking off a small piece while the rest fell to the porch.

She chewed hungrily and swallowed; the meat was fresh and flavorful. Then, she picked up the second piece in her mouth and chewed again, savoring the moment as the spices sank into her cheeks before she swallowed.

"You're...h-h-h-h-ungry...." said the man, stuttering the words, his voice deep yet soft. She looked up at him, and he was watching her. His eyes were no longer soft, and the creases of his mouth had faded as he looked upon the hungry cat with a mask of concern.

"H-h-h-ere," he said, hastily breaking off another piece of the meat and tossing it to her. Fern dipped low again, taking the piece and breaking it in two with her sharp teeth and consuming it quickly.

The man sat there against the wall watching her. Around them, the snow fell in blankets, and the grass outside the covered tavern porch grew a dusty white. Occasionally, cars would buzz down the road that separated her bridge from the tavern, paying no mind as two souls met on the old, wooden porch.

She heard the wrapper crunching as the man pulled the last piece of meat from the package and looked at it. He twisted the meat, breaking it into two pieces for her, and then tossed it gently once more at her feet. She swallowed it nearly whole, barely taking time to chew. She was still hungry, but the spiced beef tasted heavenly and went a long way to filling the growing hole in her belly.

When she had finished, she looked up at him as he leaned against the wall, watching her. He crumbled the empty wrapper and stuffed it back into his backpack, zipping it closed. Then, he slipped his black glove back on his hand and tucked his arms beneath the blanket and simply sat there, watching her. She looked back at him, cleaning her paws and waiting for more food.

"C-can't spare no more, now," he said, looking at her with an expression of disappointment. "M-maybe some other time," he said, almost sounding ashamed.

After a moment, Fern stepped backward and pressed herself through the railing of the porch and leapt to the ground, her feet making paw prints in the snow. She walked slowly and comfortably across the yard to the sidewalk and looked in both directions. The sharp edges of the tall buildings of the city at the far end of the horizon to her left were cloaked in snow, their shiny windows reflecting back the blankets of falling white powder.

WHERE THE IRISES BLOOM

She looked back up toward the tavern. She could not see the man through the railing, yet she could sense him sitting there, and she knew he was watching her. She paused for a moment and then darted across the street toward the bridge. Suddenly, the brakes of a car ground into the road, and the tires skidded hard along the wet pavement, startling Fern. A deafening horn blared into her eardrums and seemed to drive right into her skull. She leapt to the far curb in a panic and twisted herself through the chain-link and into the safety of the bridge. Then she sat there in the darkness, panting. Her heart raced.

For a long time, she did not move. She simply sat there bewildered at the violent noise that left her rattled and shaken in the darkness. Mother had warned her of the machines that moved down the roads, but in the neighborhood by the abandoned house, there were few and they moved slowly. Here, the cars seemed to whiz by, people hurrying to reach the innards of the city.

After some time, she regained herself and walked slowly down into the bowels of the bridge toward the end where the darkness met the metal wall. She pressed herself against the concrete and curled into a ball, absorbing the warm heat from the pipe through her damp coat. Soon, she closed her eyes and faded off to sleep, her belly less hungry than before.

CHAPTER 5

FERN WOKE TO the interminable scratching of the rats hidden somewhere in the darkness of the bridge. Wherever she went, the rats seemed to follow. Raising her head wearily from her paws, she could hear their jagged claws digging and scuttling against the rough concrete. Lifting her chin from the hard ground, she squinted and peered into the darkness, pressing her nose forward toward the thin vertical opening to the world beyond. Faint shafts of light poked through the gap, edging their way into the blackness of her lair. From the depth and hue of the light that slinked into the bridge, she knew the sun sat just below the horizon, reluctantly rising once more over the squalid city.

Fern rose slowly to her feet and arched her back in a deep stretch. As always, her joints were achy and sore from the unforgiving concrete. At her movements, the scratching ceased and the sounds of scurrying feet foretold the small black shadow that darted from the bridge into the cold morning. Fern walked slowly to the opening and poked her head outside. A soft blanket of snow drifted lazily from the iron-gray sky, coating the narrow strip of grass that edged the parking lot with a frosty, white blanket.

She sat there, absorbing the world for a moment. On the road that ran across the bridge, she could hear the wet spinning of rubber tires as an endless stream of cars hurried across toward the city. To her left, a sea of cars and trucks in shades of red, blue, silver, and black stretched across the parking lot as far as her eye could see. As she watched, more cars streamed into the lot like a parade of endless ants and quickly stopped, discharging their drivers in suits and ties to hustle toward their busy lives in the city. They walked past her briskly, clutching their briefcases and holding their umbrellas high against the light snow, as she sat there unnoticed in the shadow of the dead trees.

Her belly grumbled a low, deep growl. Sleep had brought respite, but in her wake, there was no escape from the pangs and cravings that coursed through her fragile body. Fern knew that she must find food today and set her mind toward the mission of satiating her hunger.

WHERE THE IRISES BLOOM

As she watched the people hustle by, their brows furrowed and lips turned downward, it dawned on her that there must be food near the big buildings where they worked. Surely, this many people needed much food to keep them bustling and busy. Where these people ate, perhaps she might find scraps and crumbs that would keep her another day.

When the flow of people passing by finally ebbed, she stepped slowly into the moist, dead grass and looked around, scanning for any signs of threats. Seeing none, she crept to the sidewalk and turned the corner, facing down the bridge toward the tall buildings that lay shrouded behind the gray clouds and the blanket of wet snow. She paused for a moment and gazed at the porch of the tavern, her eyes scanning for the man, but he was gone.

Fern started across the bridge in a hurry, wary of being so exposed on the pale concrete with nowhere to run or hide should a human come. Then, a car whistled past, and its wheels rolled through a slushy puddle, spraying the soggy mush high in the air until it rained down on Fern in a filthy, cold, brown rain. She buckled as the frigid slush doused her body and then shook herself vigorously from side to side as droplets of brown liquid splattered in dark stains on the pale concrete. Then she sprinted toward the end of the bridge, hurrying to escape the spray from another approaching car.

As she crossed the bridge, the rough concrete gave way to the stones of a red brick sidewalk. The smooth brick was welcoming to her tender paws, and she began to walk quickly toward the heart of the city, the buildings rising up on either side of her like a drab, unnatural canyon. Ahead, she could see several people in the street, standing before the open door of a shop. Three men talked loudly, gesturing with their arms and laughing occasionally. Fern slowed her pace and pressed herself against the wall of a building, hiding in plain sight just below two large, glass windows pasted with bright signs.

She looked to her left, considering her escape plans. An endless row of parked cars blocked her view of the street, but she could hear the whistling of slick tires on the pavement beyond. She sat there crouched against the wall, staring nervously at the men and waiting for them to leave. As she watched, people continued to file in and out of the open door, carrying paper bags, metal cans, or noisy plastic packages that rattled as they walked.

A woman in a long, black coat emerged from the store carrying two plastic bags, her hair wild and curled high atop her head. She started down the sidewalk in Fern's direction, oblivious to the tiny cat pressed against the wall and muttering to herself. Fern's heart raced, and she turned back toward the bridge to flee but then stopped in her tracks. Two men in their dark suits and rain slickers approached from the other direction, heading quickly toward the city. Fern's eyes grew wide, and she pressed herself against the wall. She could feel the panic setting in. She turned again toward the woman with the plastic bags who was almost upon her now. The rattle of the white, plastic bags grew louder now, and the sounds of her rubber boots on the brick drummed ominously in Fern's ears.

"Gon' cook me up some breakfast, now. That's right...." she said to no one in particular.

Fern turned back toward the men. They were just feet away now, stone-faced and grim as they marched to the tall buildings. Desperate, she stepped toward the street, daring to dart across traffic, but just then, a large truck rumbled by, rumbling the sidewalk, and she froze.

She closed her eyes and scrunched herself into a ball in the shallow doorway of a building and closed her eyes, waiting for whatever inescapable fate may befall her.

I should never have crossed the bridge again.

And then the men and the woman passed and were gone, none of them taking notice of the small cat pressed into the corner of the busy city. Fern opened her eyes and watched them fade into the distance. Looking down the block, she saw that the men in front of the store were gone and the path was clear. Without hesitation, she darted down the sidewalk, passing the store and rushing past the large, glass windows of the businesses that dotted the city block.

She reached the end of the block where the streets met and stopped. Cars and trucks zipped across her path. The road was bigger than any she had ever seen, a full four lanes of traffic. She stood there, studying the situation and trying to conjure a way she might ford the treacherous intersection.

Then, she heard feet shuffling up beside her and crouched instinctively, expecting an attack. She craned her head and looked up, the dreary sky sealed away behind the broad fabric of a red umbrella that loomed over her like a cloud. An older woman with short locks of white hair looked down at her through a pair of dark-framed glasses.

"Sweetie, you need to be careful out here," she said softly.

Fern looked up at her, studying her kind face and her dark gray business suit. The woman looked back at Fern with a look of concern on her face.

"Don't you have a home, sweetheart?" she said as she waited for the light to change. "A little cat like you doesn't need to be out here in the big city."

And with that, the clouds reappeared as the umbrella moved away as the woman stepped off the sidewalk and hurried across the street. Fern sat there on the corner for a moment, digesting the kind words of the woman.

Didn't she know I was hungry?

The sounds of traffic shook her from the fog, and she hurried across the street after the woman, but she was already gone, vanishing into the bustling crowd of people milling beneath the mighty buildings. The crowds passed her on either side, stepping sharply to avoid her, yet barely making eye contact —consumed in their busy lives.

As the sun rose higher in the morning sky and the rays of light struggled to push their way through the dense clouds, Fern set about exploring the city in search of food. She followed a crowd of well-dressed people, walking purposefully into the long shadows of a towering building of white slab concrete and shiny glass. One by one, they filed through the broad glass doors and vanished into the belly of the stoic tower. Fern hurried her pace as the doors pressed slowly together behind a man and woman engaged in conversation. Her tiny legs weren't fast enough, and the entrance sealed with a whoosh of air as the doors shut before her. She stood there, staring curiously at a portrait of herself reflected back in the polished glass. Cocking her head quizzically at the strange image, she examined the disheveled young cat who gazed back at her with pale green eyes and long ribs that arced visibly through her filthy white, orange, and black fur.

Behind her, footsteps drew near and a thick leather shoe stomped hard on the pavement, startling her to attention. "Get out of here," growled the shadowed face of a man looming tall above her as he reached for the door and pulled it open. She jumped off her back paws, springing backward as the door swung toward her suddenly. Just as suddenly, the door sealed shut, and she stood once more, staring at her meager reflection.

After a moment, she gathered herself and crept away down the sidewalk, darting and dodging the feet that stomped toward the tall building. Circling the block, she soon learned that the dumpsters and trash cans were hidden deep behind the buildings, in corners and crevices, far from the busy sidewalk. She began to venture up and down the city blocks, creeping through the alleys, as she followed her nose in a quest for food.

Behind one of the tall buildings, she found a giant, green dumpster, its broad doors opened wide. She could smell the scents of food wafting into the alley, so she leapt on a ledge of the building and jumped headlong into the dumpster, landing softly on all fours on wet, black plastic bags. There she stood atop the heaping rubbish, sniffing the air, focused on the scents.

After a moment, she located the source and

crept across the bags to one that smelled rich with food, tearing away the plastic with her teeth. With her paws, she dug around in the bag, picking away wet tissues, bits of Styrofoam, and plastic utensils until she unearthed a cardboard container brimming with half-chewed pasta, coated in a cold, red sauce. She gnawed at it hungrily, angling her head to chew off corners of the hardened noodles and lapping at the curdled red sauce with her tongue. Soon, her belly was full and her nose and whiskers were coated with chunks of tomato paste.

She sat for a long moment on the mound of trash, savoring the fullness of her belly. Then, a dark shadow cast over her, and she looked in terror up to the edge of the dumpster to see the arched figure of a large, black cat standing above her. His yellow eyes peered angrily into the garbage below.

Then, his mouth opened like a trap lined with long, white fangs that flickered in the glow of the late morning haze. A deep, horrible hissing noise brewed in his belly and spilled forth from his gaping maw. Fern's hair stood on end as she hunkered low on the plastic bags, and her body began to quiver.

WHERE THE IRISES BLOOM

The black cat roared again, a loud, shrill howl bellowing forth and filling the alley. He bared his teeth again and arched his back, his fur bristling. Against the gray clouds, his fearsome silhouette looked like some nightmare come to life. Then, he bent his legs and pounced, arcing across the sky. His black shadow filled Fern's vision as his wicked claws unsheathed and bared themselves menacingly. Without thinking, Fern darted for the opening in the dumpster. She skipped across the black, plastic bags with deftness and jumped blindly into the alley beyond just as the big, black cat landed with a thud on the bags, his claws shredding the plastic.

Fern flew from the dumpster opening and hit the wall of the building with her shoulder, tumbling awkwardly to the ground. She rolled and righted herself then sprinted away in the direction she was facing, putting distance between her and the black cat. At the end of the alley, she turned the corner and headed back for the main street, hoping the cat wouldn't follow her to where the people milled below the tall buildings.

As she came to the intersection, she stopped and looked behind her, panting. The black cat was gone, seemingly content with the remnants of the dumpster. Fern's tiny chest rose and fell, and she gasped and tried to compose herself. The sidewalk was quiet now — the masses of people safely back in their buildings. Here and there, only a few ragged souls roamed, like Fern, searching through trashcans for food.

When she had assured herself that the black cat was not coming, she started back toward the bridge with her full belly. As she walked, she craned her neck to look up at the buildings with their broad windows plastered with big, colorful signs and their doors drawn with rusted metal bars that reflected off the shiny glass. Cautiously, she stepped down the red brick sidewalk as the scant remnants of snow fell softly around her.

After a bit, she paused and gazed across the street, her eyes scanning above the cars that lined the curb. Towering high above, the dark stone of a church tower rose straight into the cloudy sky. At its peak, she could just see the edges of a black bell hidden in the wintry smog. She stared in wonder as her eyes absorbed the breadth of the church — the length of a full city block. In her earlier haste to make her way into the city for food, she hadn't noticed the church looming across the street, but now it stood there before her stoically, a cold monolith of stone and crosses glowering down at the city below.

Fern walked toward the curb and peered between two cars, taking in the enormity of the building. A black metal fence ringed the church, set in front of thick, browned turf that was much fuller than the scant tufts of weeds and sharp blades of coarse grass that sprouted through the sidewalks and on the corners of the city blocks. She gazed up and down, staring in wonderment at the colorful, stained glass windows that dotted the dark stone walls. As her eyes consumed the splendor of the strange building, they stopped and fixed on a familiar sight.

There, set in a small alcove of the church, hidden behind two bushes, she saw the edges of a familiar, olive green jacket. She studied the edges of the jacket for a minute and craned her neck slightly to the left to see around the edges of the alcove. She could see him there now — the man from the tavern. His dark winter cap was pulled low over his head, and the dusty silver-gray of his whiskers sprawled unkempt from his dark skin. Fern sat on the sidewalk and watched him for some time between the cars. His head was tilted downward, and he leaned against his backpack, reading a worn and tattered paperback book. He did not see her there watching him.

She knew he was feral, like her.

Without thinking, Fern started slowly across the street toward the church, drawn to the man. The slush of the road soaked into the crooks of her paws, and her feet grew damp as she reached the yellow lines on the road.

Bwaaaaaaaaaaaaaaaaaaaahhhhhhhhhhhhhhhhhhh hhhh!!!!!!!!!!!!!!!!

The jolting sound of the blaring car horn filled her with panic and pounded into her ears. Slick tires grinded on the wet pavement, and her body tensed suddenly, and then she shot across the street blindly. Behind her, she could hear the angry shouts of the driver muffled behind his glass window as he passed.

Her momentum carried her across the sidewalk, and she slammed sideways into the iron fence, landing on all fours in a crouch. Her body went rigid, and she shivered as if the violence of the world had awoken around her once more.

"Y-y-y-ou b-b-better be careful, friend," said the voice from the alcove. She could hear the concern in his voice. The words were jagged and awkward.

The man rose to his feet and set the book down on the steps. He stepped from the shadows of the alcove and walked across the dead grass toward her. Her eyes turned toward him and met his gaze. His look was concerned but kind as he approached unthreateningly.

"Don't y-y-ou go in that street now," he said as he drew near. "These p-p-people don't care nothing 'bout you."

Fern's tense body relaxed as she sat there on the other side of the iron fence, watching him draw close. When he was near, he crouched on the other side, his thick pants crunching as he bent down to her. He paused for a moment and let her greet him on her own terms. Slowly, Fern's nose lifted to the sky, and she inhaled his now-familiar scent.

Gently, he reached with his left hand and pulled the black glove off his right then slid his bare, calloused hand through the fence and let her smell him. She pressed her nose against his coarse skin and then slid her face down the length of his finger, scratching herself on his hand. Just barely, he smiled.

Then, his mouth opened, and he started to speak but stopped, as if he didn't know what to say. Fern rubbed her cheek up and down the edge of his hand, and a low thrumming rose from deep within her throat.

She noticed his eyes close slightly, and the corners of his mouth turned up as if some strange new feeling welled unexpectedly within him. Around her, the sounds of the cars passing faded into a blanket of quiet as she brushed against his rough hand.

Then, the quick slam of a car door broke the moment and she jolted upright. The man withdrew his hand suddenly and stood, looking toward the sound of the noise. Fern followed his gaze and saw the blinking red lights of a white car pulled against the curb just ahead. Footsteps thudded through the slosh, and after a second, a pair of legs in khaki pants stepped over the curb and approached down the sidewalk. She looked up at the man approaching, observing his bright, blue jacket emblazoned with a circular, white emblem. His skin was dark, only a shade lighter than the man from the tavern. He was younger, too. The coarse black hair on his head and around his mouth was neatly groomed, and he smiled as he approached, as if he knew the man from the tavern.

"John," he called out as he walked casually down the sidewalk toward them.

Fern sat there by the fence watching. The man from the tavern stood to full height, but he did not flee. She stretched out with her senses to touch his emotions. She could feel no tension or fear in him, only a small hint of anxiety.

"I've been looking all over for you," said the man in the blue jacket. "Should have known I'd find you here." The man from the tavern — he was called John — looked back at him and said nothing, simply watching for the other's approach.

"How are you getting along?" said the man in the blue jacket warmly as he extended his gloved hand. John looked down at his own hands as if just realizing that one was ungloved and deciding which to extend. Then he raised his bare hand, and the men shook hands.

"I-I-I'm doing ok, Malcolm," he said shyly.

For a moment, nothing further was said as the men stood there, hands embraced. Then Malcolm let go of John's hand and glanced down at Fern crouched beside the fence.

"I see you've got a friend here," he said with a smile. "Keeping you company?"

Fern stared up at Malcom. His eyes were kind and patient. He smelled fresh and clean, and she knew he was not feral like them. She sensed that John was embarrassed as he said nothing in response to the question and just stared at the ground.

"Listen, John," said Malcolm, turning away from Fern. "I know you're tired of hearing me say it, but I'd like you to think about coming in to the center."

John stood there silently and slipped the black glove back on his hand. "I know you're a tough old bird, John, but it's going to get cold out here," said Malcolm. "Winter is here now…they say it's going to be a hard one."

John looked as if he were processing the words, the wheels churning in his mind. "I-I-I appreciate it," he said. "B-b-but you know how I am," he stuttered.

Fern saw an almost imperceptible grimace cross Malcolm's face. "We've got programs to help you, John. If you'll just give us the chance," he said sincerely.

WHERE THE IRISES BLOOM

The two men stood there in silence for a long time. Malcolm looked back down at Fern as if taking his gaze from John to ease the pressure. Fern stared back at him, and he smiled nervously at her for a brief second.

After a moment, Malcolm spoke again. "I can take you there now," he said. "We can grab your bag and throw it in the car. We've got food and shelter…some counselors I want you to talk with," he offered.

John opened his mouth as if to speak, and once again, he closed it. His lower lip seemed to tremble, and his eyes looked confused and uncertain. Then he spoke. "I-I-I know you want to help me," he said. "But I'm, I'm doin' just fine now."

Fern could see the disappointment in Malcolm's eyes. He pursed his lips and then spoke. "Alright, John," he said. "I can't force you to come with me," he added. "But I want you to know that we're looking out for you, and we want to help you," he said.

"I know you d-d-do," said John. Fern could hear the relief in his tone. "I-I appreciate it," he added.

"Where are you staying these days?" asked

Malcolm, his gaze sweeping the grounds of the old stone church.

John was quiet for a moment, waiting for Malcolm to look away, but he never did. "Around these parts," was all John said.

Malcolm's face tensed, visibly frustrated at the answer. "Ok, John. If you need anything, you know where to find me," he said, reaching into a pocket of the blue plastic coat and pulling out a small white card that he extended to John through the gate. John stared at the card for a moment and then reached out with his hand and took it, sliding it into his coat pocket. Then he nodded.

Without another word, Malcolm turned and headed toward the car with its flashing lights. Before he stepped down from the curb, he paused and looked back at John, standing there with his head bowed. Then Malcolm's gaze lowered, and he looked at Fern as she sat there silently on the sidewalk watching the scene unfold. Malcolm's lips turned upward in a forced smile, and his eyes looked at her kindly, then he stepped off the curb and disappeared from sight.

As the engine started, John moved on the

other side of the gate. "I g-g-otta go now, girl," he said. "C-c-can't stay around here now." She could hear the nervousness in his voice. Then he shuffled quickly back to the alcove and picked up his backpack, slung it over his shoulder, and hurried away down the sidewalk. As he faded away in the gray, morning sky, he stopped and turned, looking back at Fern.

"B-b-e careful now, you," he said to her. His eyes connected with hers, and in that moment, her heart could just touch the edges of his lost soul as if it were her own.

CHAPTER 6

FERN NESTLED INTO the dark hole in the bridge, pressing against the thrumming metal pipes until she could feel the warmth pulse into her dingy fur. Outside, the snow had subsided, but the chill of a brisk, bitter wind whistled through the trees and pushed into the mouth of the bridge. Thick, billowy clouds drifted slowly across the night sky, shielding the moon's gaze and casting the city in a blanket of darkness.

For a long while, Fern sat there, resting against the metal pipe. Her mind wandered to the day's events — the fearsome black cat, the angry horn of the passing car, and the brief interlude with John by the church. Each time the train rumbled below the bridge, her thoughts were drawn to Percy, and she could see him, carried away in the blackness beneath the wheels of the great machine. She shuddered at the thought of his frightened eyes as he slipped from the ledge. Then she thought of Mother, lying there alone in the shadows of the playground, the rich, dark liquid seeping into the matted fur on her side. This world was a cold, callous place for a lonely little cat.

Though she closed her eyes and tried to push the thoughts away, sleep would never come. As the rumbles of the train receded into a consuming silence, she lay alone with her thoughts. Even the vigilant rats had left her alone this night, undoubtedly burrowing and scratching somewhere beyond the bridge.

In the darkness, she stood and shook the dust from her coat. Her ears filled with the sound of the bitter wind outside, and her instincts told her to stay and rest, but there was no sleep to be found this night. And so she stepped toward the edge of the bridge and entered the night world outside.

The sharp wind bristled her fur and chilled her to the core. For a moment, she stepped back into the bridge and paused. Then she looked around at the world outside, dark and solemn — the city was asleep. Dipping her head to pass through the low branches, she left the comfort of the bridge and crept beneath the trees down the edge of the parking lot, seeking relief from her thoughts.

The long pavement was vast and empty, like a still, black sea. Somewhere far from the city, the busy workers were nestled away in their warm homes and blankets. Tomorrow morning, they would be back, and once more, the city would teem and bustle with their presence.

Fern crept the length of the parking lot, circling along the metal fence that edged the main road to the north. When she reached the street, she paused. Ahead, the sight of an enormous, windowless brick stadium filled her vision. Above, a neon sign silently flashed bright, colorful images to the quiet, empty street. Hues of green, blue, and white reflected off the slushy puddles along the curb, the colors dancing eerily across the shapes of the urban landscape.

Carefully, she crossed the street and circled the edge of the stadium, peering into the large glass doors that cast her image back at her. Inside, there was only blackness. She walked across the concrete sidewalk toward the main road where four barren lanes of pavement stretched away into the blackness toward the heart of the city. Far ahead, a pair of headlights crested the hill beneath the bridge, their dim amber glow barely creasing the darkness. She sat there on the corner and watched them pass, never aware of her existence. When the noise of the car faded in the distance, she darted across the road, and her paws found safety on the concrete walkway of the other side. Never before had she been this far.

Taking a few steps forward, she stopped abruptly. The long, metal rails of the train track ran perpendicularly across her path. She stepped backward, frightened at the sight. She would not cross the tracks. And so she turned to her right, the direction the car had come, and started down the sidewalk, parallel to the metal rails.

Soon, the shadows of the overpass cast a cloak of blackness above her, and she stepped forward unsteadily, squinting to see any danger in the dark. Her ears perked, and she listened for sounds of humans or animals approaching. Hearing none, she pressed forward, darting through the shadows and out the other side of the tunnel into the dim light of the waning moon.

The lights of another car rose on the hill before her, and she pressed herself against the guardrail as the car zipped past, loud music reverberating from beyond the glass windows. As she started forward again, another pair of lights rose in the distance, veering back and forth across the lines painted in the road. She leapt atop the guard rail as the car passed, the wind nearly pushing her off the edge.

In the distance, Fern could see a tall pole rising into the black sky, adorned with a bright red and yellow sign glowing like a beacon in the night. As she stepped forward, she could see the glow of halogen lights from inside a restaurant at the base of the pole. Through the windows, she could see people milling about, their voices muted beyond the glass.

The night air carried the scent of food — rich and greasy. The smells touched her tender nose, the hunger in her belly stirred once more, and she felt a sudden purpose in her foray into the cold night. As a bitter wind blew diagonally across the road, chilling her, she hurried her pace toward the bright lights and the smells of food.

As Fern approached, people milled about the parking lot, standing by cars and talking harshly into the din of boisterous music. The doors to the restaurant opened and closed repeatedly as young people entered and left, carrying rustling, white paper bags brimming with the smells of fresh, hot food. Fern sat in the shadows and studied them, considering whether to risk venturing near the people. In the distance, she saw the familiar sight of a green metal dumpster in a concrete enclosure. Mother had taught her about the dumpsters, and she knew there would surely be food there.

All around her, car doors closed and slick tires grinded in the wet pavement, spinning then pulling away and racing down the four-lane road. Other cars entered and took their spot, and it seemed that this place was the only living place in the whole city. Fern waited until the cars had stopped and the people were all inside. She crept slowly across the parking lot, one eye fixed on the inside of the restaurant, watching for people approaching the door. Halfway across the lot, she saw a pair of women turn and hurriedly head toward the door from inside. She darted and raced towards the dumpster, finding sanctuary in the shadows before she was seen.

Above her in the dumpster, she could smell fried chicken and beef, and she could feel the saliva flowing around the edges of her mouth. She circled the dumpster hungrily, looking for the opening. Finally, she found it and crouched to leap.

"There goes that cat!" came the shout of a vaguely familiar male voice from somewhere behind her in the parking lot. Fern froze at the edge of the dumpster.

"Get that thing!" shouted another familiar voice. The chunk of ice slammed against the dumpster, shattering and spraying sharp, frozen shards all around her. One glanced off Fern's cheek, leaving a deep red gash beneath her fur.

Before she could make sense of what was happening, another chunk of ice slammed into the concrete beside her and chunks sprayed into her side, jolting her tiny body into the dumpster. She scrambled and clawed to regain her feet as ice and rocks reigned all around her.

The sounds of their laughter echoed all around her as her mind spun. Again and again, they hurled chunks of ice at her as her feet scratched on the slick asphalt to gain her footing. She stretched out to run, but her feet splayed out from under her, and she slid on her side, almost becoming wedged beneath the dumpster. In a panic, she turned and looked, wondering whether she could crawl beneath, but there wasn't enough room.

She regained her feet and darted around the corner of the dumpster just as a jagged chunk of ice slammed into the metal, the noise deafening her momentarily. Then, she disappeared into the blackness as pieces of snow and ice danced dangerously in the air all around her. Reaching the back of the dumpster, she stared up at the concrete enclosure, desperate for escape. The wall loomed high above her, far too tall for her to jump, so she crept backward into the blackness, praying that they would not come for her.

But she could hear their voices approaching from the far side of the dumpster. "Come and get it!" taunted one of them. "You gonna end up just like your momma!" shouted another. She could hear the venom in his voice.

In the blackness, Fern shivered. She pressed her body into the space beneath the dumpster, squeezing as far beneath as she could, but it was to no avail — she simply could not fit. Her tiny heart thumped in her chest and her eyes grew wide, staring in terror at the concrete wall and dumpster, searching vainly for some escape.

She could hear their footsteps pounding on the wet pavement just feet away, and the sound of their puffs of breath against the cold air pressed into the narrow space between the dumpster and the concrete wall. She crouched as low as she could and trembled, waiting for them to turn the corner.

And then, she heard his voice. "Y-y-y-ou leave that cat alone!" he shouted from somewhere far in the parking lot.

She could hear their frozen breath retract, and the space behind the dumpster grew still and quiet. The footsteps stopped. Fern's ears perked at high alert.

"I s-s-said, leave the cat alone!" shouted John, closer now. She could hear the sound of his boots approaching in the distance and then the familiar noise of his thick, canvas pants rustling.

"Who the hell you think you are?" said one of the young men, angrily. Fern could feel John drawing closer.

"Ahhhahahaa!" bellowed one of the men in laughter. "He's that old bum from downtown!" he cried in delight. The others roared with mocking laughter.

WHERE THE IRISES BLOOM

"What you doing 'round here, old man? You ain't got no money for burgers," challenged one of them.

Fern listened for John's voice, but he said nothing. She could hear him breathing, and the night air grew still and tense. In her mind, she could see John standing there before the three men, his silver-gray beard framing his dark, chiseled face beneath the black winter hat.

For a long moment, there was only silence as the men stood there on the other side of the dumpster. Fern trembled, listening but unable to move.

"That your *pussy* cat old man?" jeered one of the men. Fern could hear the spittle from his mouth as he hissed the words at John, who said nothing in return.

"You're crazy, man," said another dismissively. "You want that stupid cat? Go get it," he said. Fern could hear John's coat rustle as the man shoved him toward the dumpster.

"Better watch your back, old man." Then she heard their footsteps walking across the parking lot. Car doors closed, and the noisy engine roared to life as loud music blared behind the windows. Then the tires spun and squealed, and the sound of the music faded in the distance.

When the night outside grew quiet, she could hear him breathing. Slowly, she stepped from behind the dumpster, edging out of the shadows toward his familiar smell. At the corner of the dumpster, she turned and looked up at him. He stood there, looking down at her. His jaw was set firm beneath his grayed beard, and his eyes looked grave and serious. Without thought, she stepped from the shadows and brushed against his leg, her tail standing tall and her body edging circles around his legs. From deep within, she started to purr, and she knew he could feel it through his thick pants. He looked down at her, and his eyes softened. Slowly, he reached his gloved hand to her and stroked the length of her back. At the touch, she arched her spine to meet his him, and she could feel his smile.

"I-I gon' get us some food," he said. "Wait for me."

Then he stepped across the parking lot, his hands digging deep into his pockets. She could hear the coins jingling until he pulled the handle and stepped inside. She waited for him patiently in the shadows of the dumpster. As the cold wind blew across the pavement, she felt at peace, watching him fondly through the glass. Inside, she could see the noses of the others turn up as they stepped away from him, their faces wrenching in disgust. They let him ahead in line, and as he approached the cashier, her eyes rolled, and she glanced backward at another employee and sighed.

Fern could see his mouth moving, only uttering a few words as he moved the metal coins around in his palm and then handed them to the cashier. In a few minutes, the door opened and he was back, walking toward her with a crinkled, white paper bag. She stood as he approached and brushed once more against his legs.

"Come on, now," he said, sounding comfortable — there was no stutter this time. He stepped around the concrete enclosure and climbed a small, grassy hill, then his stiff body folded with a grunt, and he sat in the snowy grass. Fern followed him up the hill and sat beside him. He opened the white paper bag, and she could smell the scent of fresh, fried chicken.

"Got us some nuggets," he said as he focused

into the bag, lifting a small, cardboard box with his thick glove. He lifted the lid, and the rich smells filled Fern's nostrils. She was euphoric. John reached into the box with his hand and picked up a nugget, breaking it in half and setting a piece down on the grass beside him. Fern gnawed at it hungrily, chewing with her small teeth at the tender, white meat. When she was done, she watched John as he chewed the other half and returned her look. He only nodded at her then reached in the box and tore another in half and fed it to her.

And so they sat, side by side on the snowy hill until the box was empty. Fern longed for more of the nuggets, and she knew John did as well, but she was happy just the same. Her belly seemed full, and his kindness warmed her soul. They sat in silence for a long while, listening to the cars come and go from the parking lot as the drifting gray clouds blotted the moon from the sky and the cold wind blew briskly across Fern's coat.

Then, John stood and looked off into the distance of the city, his eyes looking watchful and nervous. "I-I-I got to get going now," he stuttered, looking down on her fondly. "I-I-I'll see you around the town." And with that, he crumbled the paper bag and stepped down the hill. She watched him drop it carefully into the mouth of the dumpster, and then he turned once to look at her. His eyes looked worried, and she could sense that his mind was racing, as if he was suddenly afraid. She watched him as he walked off across the parking lot until his shape vanished into the darkness beneath the bridge.

CHAPTER 7

FOR TWO LONG days, a bitter cold cloaked the city in its miserable grasp. Fern huddled in the depths of the bridge, clinging to the faint warmth of the metal pipe. Only when her tiny bladder pressed against her sides did she dare venture outside to relieve herself in the bitter cold. Even then, she pranced quickly on her toes across the frozen grass to keep her feet from sticking and squatted just outside the bridge opening beneath the icy branches of the trees. When she finished, she would hurry back into the depths of the bridge and nestle on the concrete against the pipe.

Her stomach was hungry as always; she had not eaten since John had shared his nuggets with her on the hill behind the dumpster. Each time Fern would return to the bridge, she would glance across the street toward the tavern, looking for John's silhouette against the faded bricks. Again and again, she would look, but he was never there. She hoped that he was tucked away somewhere warm. Outside in the parking lot, the morning workers bundled themselves against winter, their coats and hats revealing only slivers of their grim faces as they shuffled quickly across the frozen concrete.

On the third day, the bitter chill subsided and the pale, lifeless sun rose almost begrudgingly beyond the gray, wispy clouds. The day was cold and clear, but Fern could tolerate the temperatures now, warmer, but just below freezing. As the stream of workers trickled to only a few stragglers running late for work, she emerged from the bridge, hungry.

Once more, she circled the edge of the parking lot, keeping close to the bushes along the chain-link fence. She waited patiently at the busy, four-lane road and darted across just behind a passing truck. Ahead, the railroad tracks blocked her path to a new part of the city beyond. She paused at the metal rails, the sounds of the thundering train carrying Percy away, once again, filling her ears. The tracks were still and quiet, and she sensed no vibrations. Yet, she knew that, at any moment, the great machine may come barreling into view and sweep her away, too.

She looked up and across the tracks. The blighted city stretched for blocks — dilapidated row houses and warehouses lined either side of the street, pressing against the broken cars and piles of trash that edged the jagged and cracked concrete curbs. She sat for a minute, feeling for the vibration. The only grumbling came from her belly, though, and it led her onward, leaping over the tracks in one large pounce. As she landed on the other side, she turned toward the tracks as if they were alive, but they only lay there, cold and dead. Her heart beat quickly, but emboldened that she had crossed the tracks, she scurried to the sidewalk and started into the far side of the city.

As she walked, her head turned from side to side, surveying this new place. To her right, a giant warehouse rose high into the drab sky, its broken windows looking out over the neighborhood like an endless row of dead eyes laid upon the corpse of the city. Fern continued past the warehouse and crossed a short alley. Ahead of her, worn brick row houses lined the street, their faces dotted with peeling white-painted doors and rusted chain-link fences. At the end of the block, a woman stood alone on the corner, shuffling from side to side anxiously. Fern rested on her haunches on the sidewalk and watched her.

The woman stood there, bobbing back and forth, as if doing some awkward dance. Her mouth was moving, but Fern could hear no words. She seemed to be talking to herself — a conversation playing out in her mind. Her black coat was torn and tattered, and a thin black cap covered her head. Dark, wild hair poked from the edges of the hat as she stood there, lost in her own world, as her wild eyes scanned the street.

Then, a car pulled up to the intersection. Fern watched through the rear window as a man leaned over and spoke words to the woman. He could hear her talking now to the man. Her voice was broken and uneasy as she leaned into the window. They spoke for a few moments, and then the man reached over and opened the passenger's door. She slid into the seat like she had done it a hundred times before, smiling a hollow smile and mumbling to herself. Puffs of gray streamed from the tailpipe into the frozen air, and the car pulled away and disappeared into the drab tapestry of the city.

Fern sat alone on the block in the silence of the dead morning for a moment watching the car fade away and then stood and continued onward. As she passed the row houses, she studied the narrow alleys that lay between them, searching for signs of fresh trash bags and sniffing the crisp, winter air with her tender nose. Mother had told her that the mornings were not ideal for finding scraps. The humans threw their trash out at night or on the days when the workers did not come streaming dead-eyed into the city. But Fern was hungry, and she had no choice but to search for food this morning.

Suddenly, a chipped white door flung open just ahead, the metal screen door slamming against the iron railing. Fern startled, and her hair bristled at the noise. Before she could flee, a small boy and girl spilled forth from the door, bundled in winter coats with backpacks tight to their backs. They raced across the frozen yard and turned sharply on the sidewalk. The little boy, only slightly older, clutched the girl's hand in his — her shepherd through the city. Pink and yellow plastic clasps bounced on her braids as she turned the corner holding tightly to her brother's arm.

"I told you not to be late to school!" shouted a woman from somewhere deep in the house as the white door slammed shut behind them. The two children turned the corner and sprinted down the sidewalk, heading straight toward Fern.

She hunkered low as they approached, and then at the last moment, she darted at an angle toward the chain-link fence bordering the yard where she stood to give them clearance. The children's eyes drew wide with excitement as they saw her, and they dragged their feet to a stop, panting puffs of icy breath into the bitter cold.

The little boy looked down on her, his dark cherub cheeks bulging from the smile that creased his face. Beside him, his sister looked on in wonder, as if she had never seen a cat.

"Kitty cat," she said softly, reaching out her pink-gloved hand. Fern tucked herself against the fence, unsure of what she should do. Scared, she looked into the girl's eyes and knew she meant no harm, so she slowly stood erect and let the girl's hand meet her back.

The pink glove stroked her gently, up and down the length of her coat. The boy looked down at her, smiling, and then he released his sister's hand and dropped down to his knees abruptly, his thick pants making a chafing noise on the sidewalk. Fern jumped at the sudden movement, but then he was upon her with both hands, his black gloves clumsily caressing either side of her face, his thumbs working gently into the grooves along her nose.

"I wish we had a cat like you," he said in a whisper, gazing into her eyes. Fern dipped her head and closed her eyes, embracing the soothing touches along her nose and back.

"Leave that mangy cat alone and get to school!" bellowed the woman's shouts suddenly from behind them. The boy sprung to his feet, and without looking back, he snatched the girl's hand and off they ran, their rubber boots pounding along the pavement.

"Bye, kitty!" called the girl, turning and looking over her shoulder as she ran away. Fern watched them leave and then turned and looked back toward the door. On the porch, a woman in a blue bathrobe scowled in the distance then turned and slammed the door shut. The street grew quiet once more.

Fern continued on through the city, searching the narrow alleys for signs of food. Then, she stopped. Just down one of the alleys, she could see the battered silver top of a metal trash can lying in the alley. The edges of a black, plastic bag spilled haphazardly from the edges of the can as if some scavenger had been here. She could smell grease — fresh and fatty. She turned and looked around for any signs of danger. The city block was quiet for now, the people all gone or bundled away beyond their doors. Slowly, she crept across the thin layer of snow. Just ahead, she could see the tracks from a raccoon drawing a curved line from the backyard to the trashcan. *He must have been spooked away.* She listened for any sounds of the creature. The last thing she wanted was to tangle with a raccoon, but hearing none, she cautiously crept toward the open trash can.

Stopping just below, she lingered and let the smells of the rich grease fill her nose. She closed her eyes and imagined being inside with the humans, lapping the grease from their plates and nibbling at the large chunks of fatty meat. Then, she opened her eyes and leapt atop the closed lid of the neighboring trash can. She poked her head into the bag, and the darkness consumed her, but she followed the scents with her nose. Pushing aside moist paper towels and plastic wrappers, she found it — a tilted metal tin, brimming with bacon grease. Feverishly, she dipped her nose into the lukewarm grease and began to lap at it, her coarse tongue running along the smooth metal grooves.

Suddenly, her ears perked at a faint whimpering from somewhere in the distance. She pulled her head from the plastic bag and sat crouched on the edge of the metal trash can. Again, she heard the sound — baleful and pathetic. She licked the last remnants of grease from her whiskers and nose with a flick of her tongue and dropped to the concrete silently. Once more, a whimper carried to her ears on the cold, morning wind.

Slowly, she crept down the narrow alley toward the backyard. Ahead, the tight confines of the alley gave way to a small backyard, the dead, dry grass covered with a thin layer of snow. She poked her head around the corner of the house to investigate the source of the sound.

There, hidden from the world in the farthest reaches of the small backyard, she saw a dog chained to the rusted fence on thick, iron links. He sat there on his haunches, watching her. His yellow eyes were sad and broken, but when he saw her, she sensed a brief flicker of light pass through them. Motionless, he watched her, no longer whimpering. His cropped, pointed ears jutted unnaturally upward into the metal-gray sky. Against the blanched white of the snow, his grayish coat looked drab and dull, like the harsh winter had worn his edges until he had become nothing more than a part of the bleak landscape.

Fern stood in the shadow of the house, watching him. He watched her, too. For several long moments, they stared at each other, separated by a length of metal chain and a frozen patch of dead grass, yet trapped side by side in the human's world. Then, he rose from his haunches and stood, taking one step toward her. Fern could see the lines of his ribs, and she knew he was also hungry. Slowly, his tail began to wag from side to side as he watched her, almost inviting her to approach.

Mother bore scars from the city dogs, and she had told Fern to stay away. But Fern sensed there was no danger in this one; he was only broken — chained and hidden from the world.

He whimpered at her. His tail bobbed slowly, side to side, as if waiting for a sign that she would approach, as if he longed for their two lost souls to commune in this desolate back yard in this broken city.

Fern took one step forward in the snow,

stopping to read his reaction. He watched her with soft eyes, his tail still bobbing. Then she took another step. He whimpered once more, excited at her approach. Slowly, Fern crossed the backyard, her paws leaving gentle imprints in the soft snow. The dog tugged at the end of his chain, his thick, leather collar pulling taut into his once-muscled neck.

Just out of reach, Fern paused. Mother's warnings raced through her head, but in her core, she could feel the dog's heart and sense his loneliness, his kindness. Then, she walked forward until she was within his reach. He dipped his front legs and raised his butt in the air, giving a short, playful bark. Instinctively, Fern dipped her chin and brushed the crown of her head along the line of his cheek. He lowered his rear and lay there in the grass, savoring the affection. His eyes closed, and the two sat there, absorbed in their simple gesture, Fern running her head along the bony lines of his face.

Suddenly, there was a hard, violent knocking on the glass windows of the row house followed by muffled shouting. Fern jumped to her feet, searching with her ears for the source of the sound. Beside her, the dog rose to his feet as well, staring anxiously into the windows of the house. Fern could feel the warmth leave him, and the vigor in his yellow eyes went dim once more as the metal door rattled open.

"Get out of here!" yelled the young man's angry voice as he stepped out onto the back porch, shirtless and in a pair of shorts and sandals. "Get on!" he shouted again. Fern sprinted across the short backyard and darted into the alley.

"You supposed to be a guard dog," the man chastised the dog. "You ain't doin' me no good laying around with some stupid cat!"

Fern could no longer see the dog, but she could almost feel his spirit break. In her head, she could see his eyes close slowly and sink once more into the depths of his misery. She stood in the shadows of the alley until the metal door closed again and then waited silently. After a moment, she crept to the corner and peered into the backyard and saw him sitting again on his haunches. He saw her, but this time, he did not whimper, he simply hung his head and took a great sigh. She watched him for a moment, and her eyes traced the length of his metal chain to the fence pole. She longed to free him so that he could come with her to the bridge and they could nestle together against the warmth of the metal pipe.

Above her, a light snow fluttered down, sticking on the tips of her fur. She looked at him, but he turned his gaze slowly from her and stared blankly into the back of the house. Then, with some effort, he lowered himself to the ground, rested his chin on his paws, and closed his eyes as the snow dusted his filthy gray coat.

Fern looked at him once more, and in her mind, she vowed to him she would be back someday. Then slowly, she turned and crept out of the alley back toward the street. She walked down the block, heading in the direction of the train tracks. Her mind was with the dog in the yard, and she knew that, although she walked these streets hungry, tired and alone, she was the lucky one.

Once more, Fern bounded over the train tracks and crossed the busy street in a gap between speeding cars. She circled around the edge of the parking lot, her eyes searching the tree line near the bridge for any signs of movement near her home. As she drew closer, she squinted, seeing a shape moving near the bridge. She hunkered low and slinked along the edges of the trees, hiding herself in the shadows beneath the branches.

Ahead in the distance, she could see a large cat resting at the corner of the bridge. Her heart jumped in her chest with sudden fright. His orange coat was thick and ragged, and his large jowls gave his face a rounded appearance. Even from halfway along the parking lot, she could smell him — the unmistakable stench of the old tomcat filled the winter sky.

Despite her attempt to hide among the dead trees, he had seen her coming. He stood there at the corner of the bridge and watched her —confident but calm and unthreatening. Then his round, orange head tilted backward, and his nose rose into the air, deeply inhaling her scents. He stepped forward a pace and poked his head into the blackness of the bridge. Fern's heart pounded, and she began to panic at the thought of losing her hidden sanctuary. Then, he withdrew his head and gazed at her as she tucked herself lower toward the frozen ground.

After a moment, he began to trot down the edge of the curb. He moved almost elegantly, his gracefulness belied his filthy, almost comical appearance. As she watched him, she knew there was no sense running. The old tomcat would undoubtedly catch her, and she was clearly no match for him.

As he drew near, the cloud of his scent followed him, racing up her nostrils. She winced, her senses consumed in the overpowering pheromones. She wondered at his intent and thought about running, but she dared not leave the bridge. So she stayed there, crouched low in the snow beneath the branches.

The orange tomcat sauntered the last few paces down the curb and stood before her. His nose twitched the air again, absorbing her scents. She watched a curious expression pass across his face as he sniffed the lingering smells of the dog. Then, he circled her, pressing close against her body, inhaling at the edges of her fur. As his massive shadow blotted the sun, Fern tensed and quivered. When he was finished, he paced a few steps into the snowy grass and rested comfortably before her.

In the woods behind the playground, where the human children play — there is a group.

Mothers and kittens…young ones — like you.

She stared at him, her eyes wide and apprehensive.

WHERE THE IRISES BLOOM

There is food from the human stores nearby.

Fern stood there beneath the branches, and slowly, her fears subsided as she sensed the old tomcat meant no harm. A cold gale whistled across the parking lot, and his eyes creased to slants against the bitter wind.

Go there. They may accept you into their colony.

There is strength in numbers, young one.

She crouched before him, engrossed in his message. Mother had told her of the colonies once — the large packs of street cats who grouped together for safety. Though she knew they existed, she had never before encountered one or had any idea where to find one.

Leave this bridge.

When he finished, he rose, and his gaze connected inward with her. His once-emerald eyes were worn dull and brown, and within them, she could see the scars of a lifetime on these streets. Yet somehow, he had survived. Then, he turned and trotted down the curb toward the bridge, stopping briefly to sniff into the opening before he darted across the street and vanished like a specter into the squalid landscape.

Above her, the billowy gray clouds opened,

and darts of frozen sleet began to pelt the pavement. She stood there lost in thought, the icy pellets bouncing off her narrow spine. She wondered what would become of her and whether she would endure this world as long as the old, orange tomcat.

CHAPTER 8

THE SOUNDS OF car doors woke her, and she walked slowly to the edge of the tunnel, poking her head out into the bitter cold. Just feet away, on the other side of the chain-link fence, the faceless workers hurried around the corner of the concrete bridge and onward toward the tall buildings of the city. A chilly wind rustled the bare branches of the trees and blew the small drifts of powdery snow sideways into her lair. She shook her head as a thin dusting of snow landed on the tips of her long, white whiskers.

Comfortable in her anonymity to the shambling masses in their bland suits and coats, she stepped out to the edge of the parking lot. They had all seen her many times. Most ignored her, although occasionally, one would give a sad or kindly glance, but they never stopped their pilgrimage to the tall buildings. She slinked along the edge of the parking lot as the regular cars filtered in and pulled into their spots like a parade of dutiful worker ants.

There to her right, the slender man in the nice white car with the shiny wheels pulled into his regular spot, opened his door, unfurled an umbrella before he even rose from his seat and walked briskly toward the bridge. Three spots away was the portly woman with her dark-framed glasses, slouched against her car with a cigarette to her mouth, hurriedly sucking in the rank fumes and tossing the butt to the damp pavement. Next to her, the tired brown truck pulled in, its motor clunking noisily as it always did. The frumpy, rumpled man climbed out, umbrella-less, and waddled away toward the bridge, futilely pressing the wrinkles from his shirt with his palms.

Fern watched them all as she often did and wondered what hurried them to the city looking so haggard and tired. She did not understand what brought them here, again and again, to park their cars, slam their doors, and shuffle off across the bridge looking like a miserable lot doomed to this purgatory of the mundane. But again and again, they came. Five days a week, they sleepwalked to the city and returned late in the day, looking more tired and miserable than before. Invisible, she watched them and wondered at their strange ways.

As the frigid wind knifed unabated across the parking lot and the people trickled away in the distance, Fern stepped onto the snowy pavement, her nose sniffing at the engines. The edges of her fur sensed the warmth of the motors. Moons ago, Mother showed them a cherished secret, one reserved for the most bitter of days.

Fern circled through the parked cars, peering in the tire wells, her nose twitching at the scents of oil and antifreeze. As Mother taught her, her eyes searched for one that was warm and spacious. Beneath the old brown truck, she found it, a large gap beneath the engine. Slowly, she stood on her tiny back legs and pressed her paws on the metal pipes. The warmth coursed through her body. Without a sound, she lifted her rear legs from the pavement and disappeared, nestling into the tight crease beside the cooling engine.

For much of the morning, Fern stayed huddled in the belly of the old brown truck, allowing the heat to soak into her coat as she listened to the strange creaks and groans from the settling engine. After some time, the metal grew cold, and her tightly curled body began to ache. Stepping carefully over the rubber hoses, she dropped to the wet pavement below. The winter chill ruffled her thin coat as she slinked beneath the truck and rose to stand in the open air.

She looked around the parking lot. To the north, cars whistled by on the busy road that ran parallel to the train tracks. To the east, the drab stadium stood tall and empty, its curved roof coated with a thick layer of snow as far as her eye could see. She turned back toward the bridge, her eyes searching for something.

Since the day he shared the chunks of crispy chicken with her on the snowy hill behind the restaurant, she had not seen John. Though she had looked for him each time she ventured from the bridge, she never saw his familiar form resting against the tavern wall. Once, she had traveled to the church, hoping to find him crouched in the alcove with his worn book, but there were only shadows. She wondered what had become of him.

Curious, she walked across the parking lot toward the tavern. Perhaps she would catch his scent or some trace of him and find out where he hid. Crossing the pavement, her feet left a snakelike track of paw prints across the snowy parking lot. As she approached the bridge, her eyes scanned the withered porch for any signs of him. Drawing near the slushy street, she could see that the porch was empty — no bags, no footprints in the snow, nothing to indicate John had been there. She walked slowly to the corner of the bridge across from the tavern and searched the area for any signs of him. Toward the city, the tall buildings loomed in the distance, their towering presence muted by the grayed winter haze. Looking toward the church, she saw nothing but the rigid iron fence, its sharp points tipped in white powder.

As a car passed slowly, kicking up trails of gritty slush, she stepped into the road behind it and trotted toward the tavern, her eyes scanning the porch once more. Walking slowly up the old wooden steps, she reached the top and dipped her head around the railing to scan the length of the porch for any signs of him. She saw only a dusting of snow on the edges of the porch where the fresh powder had blown in below the eaves.

She raised her head to the air and sniffed, her nose twitching to catch his scent. Tilting her head until it was almost straight toward the porch roof, her nostrils sucked in the cold air. Just barely, she could smell him, the faint smell of his aroma, mingled with a strange, pungent sweetness. She paused for a moment, fixated on the scents to discern his location, and then she turned and trotted down the steps and around the porch to the edge of the tavern. There, she saw a buckling wooden fence, tottering as if it may fall inward on itself at any moment. She stepped along the line of the fence, smelling for him, until she came to a large gap where the boards of the fence had fallen from the cross-beams. She knew he was near.

She paused there at the edge of the broken fence for a moment, and when she was certain it was his scent, she crouched and leapt through the missing planks, landing on the hard, craggy dirt at the edge a tangled web of dead shrubs. She could hear the rustle of his thick clothes and sensed him just feet away.

"Y-y-y-ou shouldn't come back here," he said. She could sense fear in his tone. Poking her head up through the thick branches, she could just see his outline on the other side of the dry branches. Ducking, beneath them, she crawled through toward his smell, her belly dragging along the dirt. She emerged on the other side and found herself standing in a small clearing of hard, frozen dirt, bordered on one side by the decaying wall of the tavern and the other by a limp chain-link fence running atop the deep chasm with its straight, metal tracks.

All along the base of the wilted chain-link fence, a lush field of violet-blue irises pushed determinedly from the crusted snow, their petals drawn open wide as if their vibrant colors yearned to consume the malaise of the city. Against the backdrop of the barren wire fencing and crumbling bricks, the flowers stood defiantly in their splendor, untamed and unafraid. Their scent touched Fern's nostrils, and for a moment, the blighted city faded beyond the sweet, powdery essence of the lavender petals.

She turned toward the tavern and saw John resting on the hard, frozen earth, his back against the crumbling tavern wall. Their eyes connected, and she saw that John's left eye was swollen shut, his eyelid fat and bulbous, a sickly black and purple hue. His lower lip was split and scabbed over, and Fern could see hints of white pus around the edges of the scab. His cheek was swollen into a knot the size of a stone. He looked at her with his one eye, and she could sense his embarrassment.

"I'm n-n-not doin' so good, huh?" he said through a forced laugh that triggered a brief fit of coughing and wheezing. Fern lowered herself and rested without judgment, signaling to him that she would stay. John looked back at her, his lone eye studying her. In his gaze, she could sense that he was glad she was near.

"T-t-they done got me…" he said, "…those boys." And then he grew silent and stared off above the irises toward the metal tracks. Fern rose and approached him, stepping over his outstretched legs and nestled into his lap. She pressed her head against his arm, and he bent his elbow to cradle her.

With his gloved hand, John reached out and stroked the length of her coat. As he did, she pressed firmly against him, leaning her side into his stomach and then flopped sideways, coming to rest in his lap and giving herself to him completely. John looked at her with his one good eye, and she could see the sadness welled deep within him. Yet, he said nothing and only leaned down with the other hand and stroked her as if his broken soul could heal itself by absorbing the goodness within her.

The cold day passed with Fern tucked away

in the warmth of John's lap. Around mid-day, he reached out and pulled his backpack close. She could hear the zipper jingling as he fumbled awkwardly with his gloved hand.

"I-I got somethin'" he said, with barely a hint of a stutter. "Not t-the best, but it'll do." He reached deep into the backpack, searching with his one arm as his other rested softly on Fern's back, holding her in place on his lap. Withdrawing his hand from the bag, she could see he held a metal can. Lifting his other arm from her back, he slipped off the glove and dropped it on the hard dirt.

"G-gotta use my fingers," he said mostly to himself, his swollen lip seeming to fight against the hint of a smile. Then he reached his thick fingernails under the metal clasp of the can and lifted. Fern's ears perked at the popping noise as the seal broke and the rich smell of food wafted to mingle with the sweet flowers.

John set the can down beside him and reached in the bag again and pulled out a small, metal bowl and spoon. Then he sat there, scooping a heaping spoonful of baked beans into the bowl. He lifted it and set it between his legs.

"Help yourself," he said to her. Her nose

was in the bowl before the bottom touched the dirt, and she lapped at the rich juices and chewed hungrily at the tough beans. Beside her, John reached into the can with his spoon and lifted beans to his mouth, chewing slowly opposite the swollen cheek. In a few minutes, the beans were gone, and Fern licked hungrily at the remaining juices until the metal shined beneath her coarse tongue.

When she was done, she looked up at him. Faint chunks of beans were sprinkled through his wiry beard. He looked back at her gently, and she could see in his eyes that he wished he had more food. But Fern was happy and needed no more.

Together, they rested against the tavern wall as the sun dipped on the horizon and the workers shuffled back to their cars on the other side of the tottering fence, oblivious to the two lost souls just beyond their view. John reached into the bag again, and in the sound of rustling canvas, she could hear metal jingling. As he pulled a worn, paperback book from the bag, a pair of metal tags on a long beaded metal chain dropped to the frozen dirt. Carefully resting the book in his lap, he lifted them with his bare hand and clasped the small, metal plates tightly for a moment then pushed them deep inside the bag and zipped it closed.

He slipped the thick glove back on his hand and lifted the book, reaching his fingers awkwardly into the yellowed pages to find the one with a folded corner. Then he looked at her, as if making sure she was watching.

"Only got one eye to read," he said, apologizing. And then he spread the book with his hands and began to read to her. His voice was soft and clear, and the words flowed smoothly from his lips without a hint of a stutter.

Consider all this; and then turn to this green, gentle, and most docile earth; consider them both, the sea and the land; and do you not find a strange analogy to something in yourself? For as this appalling ocean surrounds the verdant land, so in the soul of man there lies one insular Tahiti, full of peace and joy, but encompassed by all the horrors of the half known life.

Fern nestled against him as he read. The sound of his voice soothed her. Although the words he spoke were foreign to her, she knew they meant something to him; thus, they held meaning to her. As the sun dipped slowly beyond the horizon of the colorless city, John read to her in their hidden sanctuary beside the old tavern until her eyes grew heavy and she fell asleep in the warmth of his lap, a soft thrumming rising from somewhere deep within her throat.

As the crescent moon kept vigil above the tavern and a curtain of cold black drew over the city, Fern woke and looked up at him. He sat motionless against the tavern wall, his one eye gazing dispassionately across the dirt toward the shadows of the railroad tracks. Fern tilted her head and rubbed into his elbow.

"Gettin' cold out here," he said, shifting himself upright against the wall, as if he had been waiting for her to wake before he moved. Fern's legs slid, and her body slipped further into the crack in his legs and touched the cold ground below.

"You can't stay out here, tonight," he said to her, his gaze looking upward into the clear night sky where a million distant stars twinkled back at them. From the ground, she could feel the rumbling of the train in the distance, and her body tensed. John sensed her fear and reached to soothe her. "Just the train," he said as he stroked her side. Then the great machine came barreling past on the tracks, the glimmering tops of long steel cars flashing by in the darkness just beyond the chain-link fence.

When the train passed, Fern stood and arched her back, stretching away the knots and aches. Then she sat again, resting between his legs and looked up at him.

"You need to get goin'," he said. She could sense his tone grow firm. "Back into that bridge...I know where you stay," he added. She didn't understand the words, but she sensed tension in the air, as if he suddenly wanted her to leave.

"Get on, girl," he said, reaching his hands beneath her and lifting her until she was standing. Then he rose to his feet, grunting at the effort. He shooed with his hand, gesturing her back through the branches and the hole in the fence.

"G-g-get on in that bridge for the night," he said. Then he stomped his foot half-heartedly into the hard dirt. Fern startled and stepped cautiously toward the fence. She didn't understand why he was chasing her off. In the lines of his face, she could sense the insincerity of the gesture. And yet she heeded him, crouching low beneath the hard branches and climbing back through the hole in the fence.

As she crossed the empty black road, she could hear the rustle and zipper of his bag. She crept to the edge of the bridge and turned the corner, waiting in the shadows. From the darkness, she watched the hole in the planks across the road, and after a short while, she saw him duck beneath the lone wooden board and climb through. He stood there by the roadside, alone in the darkness, and pulled the backpack tight to his back. He looked across the road toward the bridge where Fern lay hidden in the shadows then started toward the city as the night drew a black shroud around the tall buildings beyond.

CHAPTER 9

FERN WOKE ONCE more to the car doors slamming, as was her habit five days a week. Draped in the clinging vestiges of a long, restless night, she walked from the bridge onto the grass and rested atop the curb, comfortable now with the busy people who passed and paid her no heed. Purposefully, she looked across the road toward the tavern, her eyes scanning the peeling old porch and the hole in the tattered wooden fence for signs of John but saw nothing. For a long while after he left last night, she sat there in the blackness waiting, eyes toward the city, watching for his form in the shadows that danced at the foot of the street lights. Only when the bitter wind punished her defiance and her skin grew chilly beneath her thin fur, did she crouch into the hole in the bridge and seek sanctuary by the warm pipe.

This morning, she thought she might wait for him a bit, hoping he would come back from the city with his bag full of food he had foraged overnight. And so she sat there for most of the morning as the busy people passed her by, and eventually, their steady stream faded until only the stragglers remained, hustling down the sidewalk, pulling impatiently at their ties and jackets.

Winter lay heavy over the city. A dull gray cloud loomed atop the tall buildings like a drab umbrella, spreading its tendrils into the neighborhoods beyond the pillars of glass and steel. From the north, a harsh wind blew through the barren trees, bending the branches and snapping the brittle ends. Fern hunkered behind the concrete outcropping of the bridge, the brunt of the wind breaking against the thick stone.

She gazed toward the city, her eyes scanning the sidewalks, and then she saw him, a black silhouette moving briskly before the church. His hands clutched at the collars of his olive green jacket, pulling them toward his face to shield the bitter wind. On his back, slung alongside his backpack, was a plastic bag brimming with aluminum cans that rattled against each other, dead and hollow.

When he drew closer, she darted across the

street to the tavern. He stopped at her sudden movement for a moment and shook his head then hurried his pace to meet her at the wooden fence.

"Y-y-y-ou can't be runnin' cross the road like that," he admonished her softly, his words muffled behind the collars pulled tight across his face. She studied his face — his swollen eye still bulged grotesquely beneath the wool hat. He looked tired.

"Come on," he said, and she followed him through the hole in the fence. He reached ahead and pushed back the broken branches that snapped against each other, and the icy chunks broke from their tips and rained around her. As they entered the barren patch of dirt, the irises danced and swayed in the frigid air as if welcoming them home. John walked to the tavern wall and dropped the bag of aluminum cans to the hard ground with a noisy clatter. Fern jumped at the unfamiliar sounds and backpedaled toward the fence.

He looked at her, surprised, and then glanced down at the cans. "I'm sorry," he said, recognizing the source of her concern. She stopped, comforted by his words.

"I got a l-l-little bit of food," he said, setting down his backpack. "Not a whole lot," he added — again, a hint of apology in his tone.

She walked to him and brushed her side against the rough brick wall. The brisk winds broke against the wooden fence and the tavern. Their hidden spot offered a reprieve of sorts from the cold gales. John knelt beside her and dug in his backpack.

"Y-y-ou ever been 'round a fire?" he asked her.

She didn't answer.

From the bag, he drew a pack of matches and a bundle of newspaper. Then he stood and walked to the edge of the chain-link fence, snapping finger-sized branches from the shrub bushes that wove their way through the links above the patch of irises. As he snapped the branches, he shook the ice and water from them and rubbed them dry against his coat. When his arms were full, he walked back toward the tavern and stacked them in a neat pile against the stone wall, stuffing wads of newspaper in between. And then, he struck a match, and the fire flared from the small pile of sticks. Fern watched in amazement, the light casting her eyes aglow. John dropped the match into the pile and watched the paltry fire rise above the frozen dirt.

John watched Fern studying the fire, her eyes following the flames as they licked high into the iron-gray sky. She sat transfixed, as embers flickered from the crackling tips of branches, drifted like fireflies at dusk, then fell to the Earth and died on the cold ground. At first, she was frightened, but the warmth of the fire beckoned her, and she rested beside him, wondering at the strangeness of it all.

As the small fire burned, John reached in his bag and pulled out a small, triangular shape of cardboard. As he flipped it open, she could smell the grease and cheese, and her belly rumbled once more. He reached down, lifting the two large pieces of hard, cold pizza and broke off half of one. Then he tore the piece into small bits and scattered them across the box, the hard pieces of crust rolling like dice.

"Go ahead," he said in barely a whisper.

She dipped her head and gnawed at the bread and cheese, taking the pieces on the side of her mouth to crunch them with her molars. When she finished, he broke off more and set it down on the cardboard. There they sat in their secret place, eating stale pizza by a tiny fire.

After they ate, John pulled the book from his coat and began to read. The words soothed her, and soon, her eyes grew heavy as she rested against him, covered by the edge of his coat. In time, the fire died and the wood ran dry. A cold chill set across the frozen ground as the sun began to ebb in the horizon and night drew close.

John looked at her. "If you gonna be here, you need some shelter," he said and then stood abruptly. Her paws slid off his rough pants, and she watched him rise to his feet. "W-w-wait here," he said and then he pushed through the branches and the hole in the wooden fence.

She could hear his feet treading down the sidewalk, and then they faded into silence. She looked around at his open bag and the smoldering fire and knew that he wasn't gone for good.

In a few minutes, the branches bent, and John appeared once more through the fence, dragging behind him a cardboard box. He walked to where she sat waiting for him and set the box down. Then he dug in his bag once more, pulling out a newspaper, sheathed in a thin plastic bag.

WHERE THE IRISES BLOOM

"P-p-probably bad news anyway," he said, glancing at the bag and then looking at her with a smile. And with that, he opened the newspaper with a loud ruffle and began to crumble it into big balls. When he was done, he stuffed the newspaper in the cardboard box, doing his best to fashion a comfortable nest. He lifted the flimsy cardboard lid to show her the inside.

"H-h-how is that?" he said as he studied her reaction. Fern looked at him and then rose to her feet and walked toward the box. The dark opening and the crumpled paper drew her curiosity. Slowly, she stepped inside, her paws rustling the newspaper. She sniffed the back of the box — it smelled like mildew, but it was warmer inside. After a moment, she settled in to the newspaper and curled up, the smell of the ink masking the stench of the cardboard. When she was inside, John let down the lid of the box, and the world grew black around her, but she knew he was there, just on the other side of the cardboard. And she felt safe.

For several hours, she dozed in the cardboard box. Occasionally, she could hear John rustling in his bag or fumbling with the faltering fire outside, and her eyes would open as slits, but then she would fall asleep again. She slept for a long while until she heard a familiar voice outside.

"John," came the man's voice from beyond the fence. She recognized it. "John, can I come in?"

Fern poked her head from the box, and she saw John stand, startled at the unexpected visitor. He reached down and clutched his backpack as if he might run, but there was nowhere to go. She watched the branches bend before the fence, and in the early dusk, she could see the bright blue jacket step through into their sanctuary.

"John," said Malcom, softly. "I-I," he faltered. "I'm sorry to intrude," he said. His eyes look downward, as if he was easing the tension of the moment. As he did, he saw Fern's head poking from the box, and something passed through his eyes — a softness or perhaps a sadness — she could not tell.

"H-h-h-ow d-d-did you f-f-ind me?" asked John, stuttering deeply. Malcolm looked at him, studying his face. His eyes scanned John's swollen eye and cracked lip and rested on the deep knot on his cheek.

"What happened, John?" he asked with

concern. "Who did that to you?" Malcom's eyes furrowed. Fern sensed the anger welling in him, and she watched his fists clench instinctively at his sides.

"D-d-don't matter," was all John said, looking down at the shadows on the cold dirt.

There was silence for a long moment as the two men stared at the ground. The lid of the box weighed heavily against Fern's neck, and she stepped from the crumbled newspapers into the clearing. Malcolm watched her.

"I see your friend is back," he said, smiling to break the tension. "Looks like he's good company."

"*She*," said John firmly, correcting him. "She," he said, more softly this time.

"Sorry…*she*," said Malcolm, enunciating the words. "Does she have a name?" he asked.

John didn't answer. Fern could feel the anxiety within him, like he wanted to run and hide and be alone in this world. His eyes shifted nervously along the ground, struggling to focus. She could see his hands quivering beneath his gloves. She walked toward him and sat at his feet, her rear paws resting on the tops of his shoes. She could feel the trembling ease slightly.

"John," said Malcolm, with a sense of urgency. "It's getting really cold out here this weekend." He let the words hang in the air. John said nothing, his eyes never rising from the ground.

"They say it's supposed to get down below zero," he said. Fern could see the look of concern on Malcolm's face. She could sense the genuineness of his nature.

"Will you come with me to the center?" he asked. "Just for the weekend, maybe?" The words went unanswered and faded into a cold silence.

Malcolm started again. "We can get you fed. Get the doctors to look you over," he said, scanning the wounds on John's face once more. Then he paused for a long moment. "Get you back on your medicine, John." Fern could feel John's feet trembling beneath his boots.

"I d-d-don't want to come in," said John, barely audible. "It's…it's not for me."

Malcolm listened patiently, letting John speak. Fern felt strangely at ease around Malcom, and she knew he meant John no harm; his demeanor was calm and unthreatening.

"John," he said, the words sounding like a question. "Do you have any family we can get a hold of?" he asked, a sense of urgency in his tone.

John shook his head from side to side at the words. "G-g-got no family here," he said firmly.

"I'm worried about you, John," said Malcolm. "Man who served this country doesn't need to be out here on the streets. I want to help you," he said. John's eyes rose from the ground, and he looked anxiously at Malcolm, as if the words had somehow awoken him.

"But I can't help you if you won't let me," Malcolm added, with the slightest hint of frustration. He stood there for a long minute in silence. John's eyes sank back toward the ground, and Malcolm looked away in respect. Fern shuffled on her feet, anxious in the quiet.

"I'm going to keep checking on you, John," said Malcolm, after a long pause. "I'm not giving up on you," he added and then slowly turned and pushed his way back through the branches. Fern heard a car door close on the other side, then an engine started, wheels ground against the pavement, and the world grew quiet once more.

That night, John left again as Fern rested in the box, and once more, he returned with arms full of broken branches and torn cardboard. He arranged the branches in a neat pile, stuffing the last remnants of newspaper and strips of cardboard between them. With his matches, he lit the fire, and the flames flickered high in the sky, casting long shadows against the wall of the tavern.

Long wisps of clouds moved slowly past the full moon. Fern sat at the edge of her box, her eyes staring into the night sky, enthralled by the movement of the clouds. John leaned against the tavern wall and reached into his backpack, pulling out an old, wool blanket. He pulled his hat low and slid the backpack against the wall then settled back, using it as a pillow as he wrapped himself tightly in the blanket.

"G-g-get in the box," he said as he looked toward her. "T-t-too cold out here." She sensed the purpose of his words and crawled into the box and nestled among the newspaper, pulling herself tight into a ball. She could feel the heat of the flames filtering into the box, and soon, the space grew warm and she fell asleep.

Fern awoke to the sound of traffic on the road outside. She opened her eyes, and the bright streaks of white sky poked into her box, announcing the morning. She pressed her head against the flap of the box and looked out. John was there, packing the blanket away in his bag and pushing at the last remnants of the smoldering fire with his stick. He saw her emerge and looked at her. His swollen eye shined under the morning sun, and she could see it open just slightly, his coal-black eye shifting against the bloated skin.

"G-g-going into town…to l-l-look for some food," he said. Then he rose to his feet and slung the bag over his back. He stepped slowly toward the hole in the fence and glanced back at her. "Y-y-you can stay there if you want," he said, nodding toward the box. Then he stepped through the branches and disappeared behind the fence.

Fern pushed her way from the box out into the bitter cold. She took long, tired steps toward the chain-link fence, stretching her legs along the way, and then crouched, emptying her bladder in the powdery snow. She circled back toward the tavern wall and sniffed near the fire. Finding a slushy puddle beside the blackened sticks, she lapped at the water until the puddle ran dry, and her tongue brushed on the moist dirt.

Then, she stepped through the branches and out onto the sidewalk. She hadn't been into the bridge in more than a day, and she thought she might visit before the persistent rodents overran her abode. As she walked toward the curb, she saw a movement to her right and turned to look. At the corner, the orange tomcat approached, gliding effortlessly along the sidewalk in plain view without a care in the world. She could smell him from some distance. As he approached, she sat and waited for him by the corner of the porch.

The cat drew near and stopped several feet from her, giving her space. Her nose sniffed the air, and she caught a foreign scent, a hint of disease or rotting flesh that she had not noticed the last time they met.

You smell my wounds.

The orange tomcat looked at her knowingly.

Every day is a battle to survive.

Fern studied his stoic face. He showed no signs of pain or sickness.

She sat there on the sidewalk in the tomcat's shadow. In his filth and decay, his spirit was somehow majestic against the blighted city. In the depths of winter in this dead city, he had managed to survive against all odds. She wondered where he came from, whether he had once been someone's cat or whether he had always been on these streets.

Go to the colony. You will not survive alone, young one.

And with that, he turned and walked back down the sidewalk and vanished around the corner of the tavern. The rotting scent of flesh followed and soon faded into the cold morning air. Fern sat for a moment, staring at the empty sidewalk, and then she crossed the street and entered the gap in the bridge, nestling against the warm pipe.

I am not alone.

CHAPTER 10

FERN RESTED IN the tepid warmth of the bridge for most the day, napping occasionally, but mostly awake and listening to the sound of the rats scuttling across the concrete floor. Occasionally, she would spring to her feet and lurch at their fleeting shadows, but they were always one step ahead, vanishing into the catacomb of the bridge.

As the curtain of darkness drew over the city, she uncurled herself and walked to the edge of the parking lot where she sat alone in the bitter cold, watching the last traces of sun fade over the drab, rounded roof of the stadium across the street. In the distance, she could hear the shrill wailing and the rattling of metal trash cans — two feral cats battling somewhere over scraps of food.

Her mind wandered to the orange tomcat. She wondered if it was he who howled in the early dusk, fighting to survive in some dim back alley of this forsaken city.

Should she seek out the colony that he spoke of? Should she abandon this bridge for safety of others? What would become of John?

The thoughts weighed on her heavily as the bitter wind blew sharply across the parking lot, rustling the dry branches and setting a thin plastic bag to flight in the sky like the tattered sail of some long-dead vessel.

In the distance, the sharp blare of the train klaxon sounded, and a single white light rose from the west, churning down the dim tracks toward the nearby station. At the intersection, the long gates flickered with flashing red lights and lowered, their mechanical arms ever tireless. Fern watched the train as it passed the gates. She could see the dim glow of lights inside and the sparse silhouettes of weary travelers, lifeless as their plastic chairs. As the train rolled into the distance, the muted quiet of a snowy winter settled back over the city.

She stared across the empty parking lot. No cars had come this day, and she knew that none would come tomorrow. She had long since figured out that the cars came five days in a row and then were gone for two. Today was the first of two days that the busy people would be gone.

On the days when the lot was empty, she did her best to keep to the curb and grass that edged the lot. The parking lot was too big and vast for a small cat, and there was nowhere to hide should she encounter some unsuspected threat.

She cast her eyes across the street toward the tavern, not expecting to see John on the porch. She twitched her nose in the sky, smelling for the telltale signs of his fire that would let her know he was back. Yet, she smelled nothing. *He must still be scavenging in the city.*

Bored, she trotted across the street toward the hole in the fence. She stepped over the wooden plank and poked her head in the opening, peering through the brittle branches. In the faint remnants of light, she could see her cardboard box resting against the old brick of the tavern — the home he had made for her. The charred branches from the fire the night before rested untouched in the shallow hole in the dirt that John had dug.

When she assured herself that John was not back yet, she nimbly leapt back out of the hole in the fence and started aimlessly down the sidewalk away from the bridge. In the back of her head, the colony called to her. She could not escape the thoughts of the large group of cats living together — many mothers and their young. The orange tomcat had told her she may be accepted there, but she would need to visit often to let them know of her and so they may come to trust her. And so, with little more to do until John returned, her curiosity propelled her onward, and she wandered down the sidewalk, unnoticed by the occasional car that passed beside her on the darkened street.

As she reached the next block beyond the tavern, her ears perked, and she stopped in her tracks, listening. From the shadows of a narrow alley just ahead, she could hear a rustling noise, like something digging in the trashcan.

Wary of startling a raccoon or another cat, she edged quietly to the opening of the alley and looked inside. Her eyes squinted, and she focused intensely into the blackness. There, sitting on the ground with his back leaning against the wall was a disheveled man. His legs clad in worn and faded blue jeans slid and twitched back and forth unnaturally across the hard concrete. Fern's eyes followed the legs up the wall.

His right arm was crossed over his body toward his left, and his quivering finger fumbled to press the plunger on a syringe jabbed haphazardly into his arm. As he did, his eyes rolled back grotesquely in his skull, and his head lolled forward and back, emerging from the shadows just enough for Fern to see an unkempt brown beard overtaking his gaunt, wind-weathered face. She stood there and watched him, frightened yet hypnotized by his strange movements.

Suddenly, he pulled his hand back, and the syringe dropped to the pavement, clattering on the concrete in the cold, quiet night. His chest began to rise and fall as he breathed rapidly. Fern could see the sweat beading on his forehead then roll down his cheek and vanish into the wiry beard. He leaned his head back against the wall, and his jaw opened and he rested there, as if breathing in the rotten soul of the world.

Fern stood there on the sidewalk for several minutes and watched — her trek toward the colony suddenly forgotten in the distraction. Eventually, his eyes opened, and he stared straight ahead into the dark wall across the short alley. Reaching over to rub his left arm, he muttered to himself and tried to stand. As he did, he tottered and fell roughly against the wall and then struggled to right himself.

Fern stepped away from the alley as he stood, crouching in the shadows of a concrete stoop nearby. Suddenly, a familiar voice called from the other block.

"John!" shouted Malcolm. Fern turned to look and could see the glow of headlights from the white car pulled next to the curb before the wooden fence. Her eyes grew wide, and she started toward Malcolm but then stopped as the man emerged from the alley stumbling and stood at the edge looking toward the sounds of Malcolm's voice. He stood there, half covered in shadow, and adjusted his tattered winter coat, fumbling with the zipper and looking as if he might fall over. Fern could see the sickness in his eyes as they tried to focus on the sounds in the distance.

"John! If you're around, I have some things for you…" called Malcolm, yelling over the fence. In the darkness, Fern could just make out his familiar blue coat as he stood near the opening of the fence, peering his head to look through the branches. He turned and glanced toward the parking lot, realizing that John was not behind the fence.

"…a sleeping bag, some food," he called out to the darkness, hoping that John was near. "Should get you through the night," he said.

Malcolm stood there, his eyes searching for any signs of John. Fern looked toward the man in the alley. Seeing Malcolm, he stepped back into the shadows and the blackness consumed him whole. She stepped one leg forward tentatively toward Malcolm and could feel his eyes look down at her, but he did not move. Then she darted across his path and ran down the sidewalk as fast as she could.

As she ran, she could see Malcolm step through the hole in the fence, his hands full. Just as she crossed before the tavern, he vanished into the hole, and she could hear the bushes rustling as he passed through to their secret campsite. She sprinted as fast as she could and leapt over the opening of the fence, rushing through the bushes into the dirt patch.

Malcolm turned, startled at the noise. As he saw her, the fear left his eyes, and even in the darkness, Fern could see a warm smile cross his face.

"Well, well. Look who's here," he said as he

set a sleeping bag and a paper sack down on the dirt beside the charred branches of the fire pit. "You're doing a better job taking care of John than I am, apparently," he said, lowering himself to greet her in a crouch.

Fern trotted toward him and lowered her head, rubbing her cheeks and the crown of her head against the inside of his legs. He stroked her gently along the length of her back and then reached under her chin with his palm and cradled her tiny face. She lifted her head and looked up at him. His dark eyes were warm and welcoming, but there was an unmistakable sadness in them. She knew his eyes had seen the worst this world had to offer.

"I didn't forget about you, either," he said. "Brought some food for you in the bag there. Some stuff for fleas, too," he added, nodding over his shoulder toward the paper bag. "Keep you from itching out here." His eyes never left hers as he spoke.

Fern didn't know what Malcolm said, but the words were warm and kind, and she knew without question they came from his heart. From deep within her throat, she began to purr, and for a long moment, she sat there with him in the dirt clearing, consumed in the simple affection of this man she barely knew.

Then he rose to stand with a soft grunt and looked down at her. She stood before him and looked back at him. "You take care of him, tonight. I'll be back in the morning to see if I can talk some sense into him again." He reached down and stroked her once more across the crown of her head and then stepped through the branches and disappeared on the other side of the wooden fence. Fern followed, trotting after him down the sidewalk as the car door closed. A small puff of smoke plumed in the frozen air, and the white car pulled away, the bright tail lights fading to tiny specks of red as they disappeared down the street.

She stood there in the cold, gazing longingly toward the church, hoping that John would soon come to see what Malcolm had left for them. Then, behind her, she heard erratic footsteps pounding on the pavement, and she turned, startled. The looming shadow of the man from the alley stumbled quickly toward the hole in the fence. She arched her back and scuttled backward in fear away from the shambling silhouette.

WHERE THE IRISES BLOOM

As he stumbled to a stop at the opening of the fence, she could hear the rasping of his labored breath. He leered at her, and she hissed, arching her back toward the sky. With depraved, glassy eyes, he stared at her, and his lips turned upward in an ugly snarl. Without a word, he turned and pushed his way through the branches. Fern stood there helplessly. Behind the fence, she could hear him lifting the paper bag, and soon, the branches bent again, and he emerged, carrying the paper bag in his left hand and cradling the sleeping bag in his right.

He looked left toward the church and then glanced down at her again, his mouth gaped open. She could smell his putrid breath on the cold air, and his gray teeth smiled at her.

"Tell your old man thanks for the stuff," he said bitterly and then laughed a malignant laugh as he hurried away down the sidewalk, vanishing around the corner.

Fern stood there watching him until he was gone. When she could no longer see him, she turned and looked toward the parking lot and then toward the church, confused. *Why had he taken their things? Where had Malcolm gone?*

She stood there in the cold until the unforgiving winds drove her back through the fence in search of the lingering remnants of John's comforting smell near the campsite. As the last vestiges of sun faded below the horizon, she sniffed around in the dirt where the paper bag had been. She could smell the faint scents of food that had rested so briefly on the ground, and her belly grumbled.

Circling the campsite, she looked in the bushes and by the fence, hoping that perhaps Malcolm had left something else behind, hidden among the lavender flowers. Slowly, she realized there was nothing and wearily climbed into the cardboard box and curled herself into a ball among the crumbled newspaper. She stared aimlessly beyond the opening of the box, waiting listlessly for John to return.

As night settled in, she finally heard the bushes rustle, and she startled from the box, poking her head toward the opening. She could smell him before he passed through the bushes, and she rushed out to greet him.

"H-h-ello, lady," John said warmly, oblivious to the intruder. He dipped his shoulder and slipped the heavy backpack off, dropping it to the ground. "I been gone a long time, I know," he said, reaching down with his gloved hand to scratch under her chin.

Fern pressed against him urgently, longing to tell him of Malcolm and the foul man who had come and taken their things. But she had no words that he could hear.

"I-I-didn't find a whole much," said John, sounding embarrassed. "But, I got a few things," he said as he reached into the bag and pulled out a white paper sack.

"Got a whole bunch of b-bagels," he said, resting the sack on the ground beside her. She could smell the stale bread through the thin bag. "B-but you not gonna eat those, I know," he said, still digging around.

Fern raised her head at the pungent scent of meat rising from the bag. "Got you these," he said, opening a small red and white cardboard box and resting it on the ground. Fern stood over the box as the scent of spicy chicken filled her nose. "I-I tried to wipe off the sauce," he added. Her eyes scanned the box, looking at dozen, tiny chicken wings, half-chewed and tinted red with the residue of some pungent sauce. Her eyes watered from the spices, but in hunger, she dipped her nose into the box and began to chew at the remnants of the meat, pressing down with her paws on the bones and pulling small chunks into her mouth. John rubbed her coat with his gloved hand as she ate and then stood and began pulling branches off the shrubs by the chain-link fence.

When Fern finished, she looked up. John was arranging a small pile of sticks on the fire. "Gonna be a cold night, friend," he said, his eyes scanning the bushes for more branches. Then, he walked toward the fence, his fingers tracing the edges for loose boards. Fern could hear him tugging, and after a moment, he returned with a small board from the corner of the fence and rested it carefully across the fire. He dug into his backpack once more and retrieved a small piece of cardboard, stuffing it under the edges of the branches. As the tiny flame of the match illuminated the outline of his face, Fern looked at him adoringly. Her world was complete.

The cold night settled in over their campsite. The bitterness chilled Fern to her bones. John sat on the dirt and rested against the tavern wall, his hat pulled low and his coat drawn high over his chin so she could only see the edges of his gray beard and his dark shadows of his face. He dragged the backpack toward him across the dirt and tugged at the edges of the blanket, unrolling it and wrapping himself tight.

Fern studied his face. The flicker of the campfire danced in his dark eyes as he watched her standing there, undecided whether she should go in the box or crawl on him.

"Why don't you come here?" he asked, beckoning with his hand. Without pause, Fern approached him, and he lifted the blanket. She stepped two legs on his lap, and he lifted her gently and cradled her between his legs then pulled the blanket around her snuggly, so only her tiny face showed itself to the night sky.

Then, he leaned over and pulled the paperback book from his bag. His thick gloves fumbled at the pages until he found the dog-eared one and opened the book. He began to read.

There is a wisdom that is woe; but there is a woe that is madness. And there is a Catskill eagle in some souls that can alike dive down into the blackest gorges, and soar out of them again and become invisible in the sunny spaces. And even if he for ever flies within the gorge, that gorge is in the mountains; so that even in his lowest swoop the mountain eagle is still higher than other birds upon the plain, even though they soar...

His voice soothed Fern, and the words embraced her spirit like a song in the bitter night. Beyond the hole in the fence, the city slept in their warm beds, yet as she rested against the rough canvas of his legs in the meager warmth of their makeshift fire, she was at peace.

For a long while, John read to her. His voice was smooth and clear, and his words flowed without a stutter. When the fire began to dwindle, John rose, shifting Fern carefully onto the blanket. He piled on the last of the branches and struck another match, lighting the cardboard. Short, orange flames licked at the sky against the cold night. Fern watched them rise, and her eyes followed the long tips as they sparked and then faded to blackness under the watchful stars.

John walked back to her and slid down the wall until he was seated beside her. She could see the worry in his eyes and noticed a nearly imperceptible shiver course through his body. He reached up a gloved hand and unzipped his thick, winter coat and then carefully scooped her up. She gave herself to him, hanging limply in his hand, and he held her before him as their eyes met in the light of the campfire.

His lips quivered for a moment and then he spoke. "Thank you," he said softly, and she thought she saw a tear forming in the corner of his eye as he tucked her into his jacket then lay flat on the ground with his head on the backpack. She heard the zipper slowly close above her, and she sank into the soft fabric of his musty, old sweatshirt. Soon, the warmth consumed her like nothing she had ever felt from the metal pipe. She closed her eyes in the blackness, and they began to breathe as one, their bodies rising and falling in perfect harmony. Then she drifted off to sleep.

In the morning, she woke to the muffled rustling of branches on the other side of John's coat. Her eyes opened, and she squinted into the darkness, listening. She braced herself, waiting for John to shift and rise, but he did not.

"John." She could hear Malcolm's voice outside, sounding urgent. "John," he said again. Fern squirmed under the coat, hoping John would wake so she could greet Malcolm. Then, something made her pause, and she waited for the rising and falling of his chest, but there was none. Beneath the sweatshirt, she could feel his body, cool and still. Frantically, she squirmed and wiggled, pressing upward against the coat.

"John!" came Malcolm's voice, yelling from just above her. She could hear him crouching down beside them, and then John's body jerked suddenly as Malcolm tugged at his shoulder to wake him. "John!" he cried, his voice now trembling. She squirmed again and let out a cry. Then the zipper pulled back, and the pale, lifeless sky spread out above her like an empty canvas.

As she poked her head from the coat, she looked up into Malcolm's face. His eyes were painted with a bitter sadness, and his mouth gaped open in disbelief. He glanced down at her, wriggling to free herself from John's thick jacket, and she could see the tears welling in the corners of his eyes. Then he lifted his head and stared straight up into the sky and began to sob, his shoulders rising and falling as the tears streamed down his face and soaked into her fur.

Fern pushed her way free from the coat and stepped gingerly up John's chest until she could see his face. His eyes were closed, and his once dark, cocoa skin now carried a bluish hue. Against the faint rays of morning light, slivers of ice sparkled and glimmered around the edges of his beard.

Unclenching his hand from John's shoulder, Malcolm pressed at his eyes with his knuckles, pushing the tears aside until they ran down his cheeks and fell in tiny droplets to the frozen ground. Then, he leaned forward reverently and grasped the edge of John's black cap, pulling it down slowly over his face. Resting softly on John's still chest, Fern watched, bewildered, as the dark cloth of the hat stretched over his eyes like a shroud.

Malcolm paused for a moment, crouched beside John with his head bowed and eyes closed. Fern watched the movement of his lips, but she could hear no sounds. When he was finished, Malcolm slowly stood as if his spirit weighed heavy upon him. As he rose, he lifted Fern gently in his hands and cradled her close against his chest. He stroked her coat and began to cry once more, the warm tears rolling down the smooth blue plastic of his jacket.

Above them, thin ribbons of gray clouds drifted slowly across the winter sky toward the city. Beyond the old wooden fence, the sounds of cars passing along the slushy street seemed to yield to a still, peaceful silence. And along the chain-link fence, just before the great chasm with its straight metal tracks, the irises stretched their amethyst petals skyward to kiss the morning sun and greet the world anew.

For a long moment, Malcolm simply stood there in the middle of the hidden sanctuary, pressing Fern tightly against his blue jacket. Above her, she could hear his mouth open and the hints of words forming as he struggled to speak.

"I'm sorry I couldn't save him," he said to her, his voice choking. "But I'm glad he had you." His voice trailed off into his tears.

Then he tucked her deep into his blue coat to shield her from the branches and pushed his way beyond the old wooden fence. With slow, shuffling steps, he walked to the white car parked at the curb and opened the door, drawing her from his jacket. Then ever so gently, he rested her on the soft fabric of the seat.

"I won't lose you, too," he said softly as he closed the door.

THANK YOU

Thank you for taking the time to read this book. If you found this reading worthwhile, please consider leaving a review wherever you purchased the book. More reviews will help more readers find and appreciate this story.

If you would like to explore my other books and receive a free short story based on the events of "Chasing the Blue Sky," please visit www.lomackpublishing.com

Thank you again for giving your valuable time to read this book. I hope you found the time well-spent.

~ Will Lowrey

ABOUT THE AUTHOR

Will Lowrey is an attorney and animal rights advocate from Richmond, Virginia. He holds a Juris Doctor from Vermont Law School and a Bachelor of Science from Virginia Commonwealth University. For close to two decades, both before and after law school, Will has been actively involved in animal causes. His experiences include deployments to assist animals in disasters, the closure of roadside zoos, caring for animals from dog and cock fighting cases, community outreach for low income pet owners in areas ranging from urban neighborhoods to Native American reservations, animal rights protests, animal sheltering, public records campaigns against large institutions conducting animal research, and countless other adventures.

In 2018, Will founded Lomack Publishing to promote the rights, interests, and dignity of animals through self-published literature. Will is also the author of "Chasing the Blue Sky," "Words on a Killing," and "Odd Robert" through Lomack Publishing as well as "We the Pit Bull: The Fate of Pit Bulls Under the United

States Constitution" published in the Lewis and Clark Animal Law Review Journal, Volume 24, Issue 2.

While most of Will's writing focuses on animal causes, he has dabbled in other areas, writing "Simple Strategies for the Bar Exam," a guide for law students and attorneys taking the bar exam, as well as "The Tenebrous Mind," a collection of horror stories.

Will enjoys hearing from readers. If you'd like to contact him, please visit:

www.lomackpublishing.com

Made in the USA
Monee, IL
23 July 2021

74199713R00104